"I'm so sorry!"

Annabel quickly wound the dog's lead around her palm. "Here, let me help you!"

Dropping to her knees, she started grabbing the loose pages and the manila folders, but the man in front of her mirrored her actions. Their heads collided with a resounding crack.

Annabel swore and fell backward, landing on her butt. She rubbed hard at the stinging at her temple, hoping to erase the pain.

Suddenly, the warmth and strength of male hands, one capturing her rubbing fingers and the other cupping her jaw, caused a shiver to dance over her skin.

"Look at me. Are you all right?"

Annabel blinked hard as her world tilted. She could swear she saw a dizzying array of stars.

Forcing her gaze upward, she found icy blue eyes, serious and probing and perfectly matching his shirt, staring intently back at her.

Forget the stars.

This was a full-blown meteor shower.

Dear Reader,

Have you ever met someone who seemed to show up in your life just when you needed them? Well, Dr. Thomas North might not realize it, but he's been waiting for Annabel Cates, and her beloved golden retriever, Smiley, all his life. What he's going to do with this vivacious blonde spitfire, her pup and the upheaval they cause to his well-ordered days is another question!

From the moment Annabel literally runs into the sexy and serious doctor, she knows what this man needs is a strong dose of love, both the human and puppy variety. Finding ways for these two very different, but perfectly matched people to fall in love is what made this story so much fun to write!

Being a fan of the Montana Mavericks for years, it was an honor to be asked to be a part of this amazing series that pays great tribute to the heart-and-home creed of Harlequin Special Edition with the wonderful families of Thunder Canyon, Montana.

I hope you enjoy their journey to happily-ever-after and please visit me at www.christynebutler.com or email me at chris@christynebutler.com!

Christyne

PUPPY LOVE IN THUNDER CANYON

CHRISTYNE BUTLER

HARLEQUIN®

entertain, enrich, inspire™

Special thanks and acknowledgment to Christyne Butler
for her contribution to the
Montana Mavericks: Back in the Saddle continuity.

Recycling programs
for this product may
not exist in your area.

ISBN-13: 978-0-373-65685-1

PUPPY LOVE IN THUNDER CANYON

www.Harlequin.com

Printed in U.S.A.

Books by Christyne Butler

Harlequin Special Edition

†*Fortune's Secret Baby* #2114
Welcome Home, Bobby Winslow #2145
Having Adam's Baby #2182
**Puppy Love in Thunder Canyon* #2203

Silhouette Special Edition

The Cowboy's Second Chance #1980
The Sheriff's Secret Wife #2022
A Daddy for Jacoby #2089

Harlequin Books

Special Edition Bonus Story: The Anniversary Party—Chapter Four

*Welcome to Destiny
†The Fortunes of Texas: Lost…and Found
**Montana Mavericks: Back in the Saddle

Other titles by this author available in ebook format.

CHRISTYNE BUTLER

fell in love with romance novels while serving in the United States Navy and started writing her own stories six years ago. She considers selling to Harlequin Special Edition a dream come true and enjoys writing contemporary romances full of life, love, a hint of laughter and perhaps a dash of danger, too. And there has to be a happily-ever-after or she's just not satisfied.

She lives with her family in central Massachusetts and loves to hear from her readers at chris@christynebutler.com. Or visit her website, www.christynebutler.com.

To the ladies at WriteRomance, the best critique partners in the world: don't know what I would do without you!

And to Susan, Charles and Jennifer…you all know why

Chapter One

"Do you understand everything we talked about during the drive here?"

Annabel Cates pulled into an empty spot in the Thunder Canyon General Hospital parking lot. "I know these visits are routine by now, but it's important we cover the dos and don'ts every time."

She cut the engine, turned to the backseat of her practically new lime-green VW Bug and was rewarded with a sloppy kiss.

"Smiley!" Annabel pushed at the wet nose of her three-year-old golden retriever, her constant companion since she'd brought him home from the local shelter when he was just a pup. "You could've just nodded!"

An excited bark was her pet's answer.

"Yes, I love you, too." Releasing her seat belt, Annabel grabbed her purse and Smiley's leash and got out of her car, pausing to hold the driver's seat up to allow her dog to exit.

Kneeling, she latched the leash on to his collar then straightened the bright blue bandana around his neck, her fingers lingering over the black lettering on the material. "Just think, buddy, a dozen more sessions and we can switch this In Training bandana for one that reads Certified."

Smiley did the exact thing that earned him his name: he smiled. Many told her it was the natural curve of his mouth, a trait common in golden retrievers, but Annabel could tell when her fur baby was happy.

Which was just about all the time.

Smiley's outgoing, friendly personality, to both humans and other animals, made him a great therapy dog. The two of them had completed the required training, registration and certification over the past few months, but the American Kennel Club required fifty visits before being awarded the title of AKC Therapy Dog.

And Annabel wanted that title for Smiley, which didn't explain this particular visit.

"But this one is special, isn't it, boy?" Annabel gave Smiley a quick scratch to the ears then rose, and they walked across the hospital's parking lot.

Once inside, she stopped at the directory near the elevators. The geriatrics and children's areas were the most familiar to her and Smiley, but today they were headed for a specific doctor's office.

Smiley padded along beside her, staying right at her knee, despite the comments, grins and hellos that greeted them. Then a little boy sitting alone on a bench came into view and Annabel felt the familiar tug on the leash.

Almost by instinct, Smiley was drawn to those who were injured and hurting, but not all injuries were visible. A low whimper and the quickening of his wagging tail made the little boy look up. The beginnings of a smile crossed his face. Annabel slowed and allowed Smiley to work his magic.

After a few minutes visiting, Annabel continued on her way, energized by the boy's improved mood and excited chatter to his mother. They stopped outside the elevators and she eyed the hospital directory on the wall.

"Can I help you?"

Annabel turned and found a pretty nurse standing beside her dressed in scrubs, a short-sleeve shirt and loose cotton pants featuring a dizzying pattern of colorful flip-flops. Perfect for a warm August morning in Montana. "Yes, I'm looking for Dr. North's office."

The woman's eyebrows rose, disappearing into her perfect straight bangs. "Dr. Thomas North?"

"If he's an orthopedic surgeon, then yes, he's the one."

"Is Dr. North expecting you?" Her gaze shifted to Smiley for a moment. "Both of you?"

Living by the motto "it's better to beg for forgiveness than ask for permission," Annabel smiled. "We're here to visit with one of his patients."

"Oh. Well, his office suite is on the second floor, far left corner. I could show you if you'd like."

"That would be great, thanks."

The elevator dinged and seconds later the door opened. Annabel and Smiley waited for everyone to depart before they followed the nurse inside. Once on the second floor, they turned a few corners and moved into an office area. At the end of the long hallway Annabel finally spotted the nameplate for Dr. Thomas North.

"Hey, Marge. I've got a visitor for you."

The older woman sitting behind the desk was obviously Dr. North's secretary. Annabel smiled, not missing the glances between her and the nurse or the way her eyebrows rose in matching high arches, as well.

It was okay. She and Smiley were used to it.

"Can I help you, miss?" Marge asked as a beeping noise filled the air.

"Oh, shoot. I've got to go." The nurse checked her pager and smiled. "I so wanted to stick around and see this. Let me know what happens, okay?"

Marge gave her a quick wink and nodded.

A bit confused, Annabel offered her thanks. The nurse waved it off and then disappeared.

"Miss?"

Annabel turned back to the woman. "Oh, I was wondering if Forrest Traub has arrived for his appointment with Dr. North yet?"

"And you are?"

She opened her mouth to reply, but a low, measured voice came from over her shoulder.

"What are you doing here, Annabel?"

She whirled around, surprised to find the man she'd asked about had somehow snuck up on her. Not usually easy to do with Smiley close by. Annabel then noticed her dog remained sitting at her side, perfectly still, not even his tail moving as he stared intently up at Forrest.

And there was a lot to look at.

Tall, muscular, dark hair and the coolest light brown eyes. Yes, he was very nice to look at. Annabel was sure her sisters would use words like *yummy* and *sexy*. Even the two recently married ones, one of whom was the bride of Forrest's cousin, Jackson, would have to admit good looks ran strong in the Traub family tree.

Too bad the man did nothing for Annabel. No spark, no fizzle.

But that was fine with her. Annabel wanted more. She wanted true love.

The kind of love that came at you like a bolt of lightning and left you dazed, confused and tingly all over. She'd never felt that way in her life, but darn it, after a dry dating spell that had been going on for three years, she was ready for it!

"Hello?" Forrest leaned heavily on a cane with one hand while waving the other in her face. "Annabel?"

"Oh, sorry!" She blinked hard and chased away her dreams. "I…um, I'm here to see you."

His mouth pressed into a hard line as he looked down at Smiley. Annabel did the same, noticing how her pet returned the man's stare with a simple tilt of his head.

She wasn't sure who was sizing up whom.

"How did you know I was going to be at the hospital this morning?" he asked.

Her cheeks turned hot. "I overheard you talking to Jackson at the family barbecue yesterday."

He opened his mouth to say something, but Annabel kept talking. "I know you've been through so much since you got back from overseas. Even before then. And after all that time you spent at Walter Reed Medical Center to still need…well, I thought we could help."

Forrest sighed and directed his gaze to the secretary. "Would it be okay if I—if *we* waited for the doctor inside his office?"

A thrill raced through Annabel. It wasn't a complete victory, but it was a start.

"I'll take full responsibility for them being here," he continued. "And I really need to sit down."

The woman's blue eyes flickered toward the chairs in the corner of the room, but then she said, "Of course, please go in. The doctor is running late, but he should be here soon."

Forrest gestured toward the open doorway with a wave of his hand. Annabel gave a quick tug on the leash and entered the office, Smiley at her side. Forrest followed, and the doctor's secretary stood to close the door behind him.

It was a large room, with a wall of windows behind tightly closed blinds. Two chairs sat in front of a large desk with a more comfortable-looking leather couch along one wall.

Annabel stayed off to the side, not wanting to get in Forrest's way as he dropped into the closest chair. He jammed the cane she didn't remember him using yesterday into the armrest and closed his eyes. His right leg stuck out straight. The bulk of the brace underneath his jeans pulled the worn denim tight around his knee.

This time Smiley tugged a bit at the leash and Annabel released the slack, allowing the dog a bit more leeway while keeping a tight grip on the looped handle. Just in case.

Smiley had been with her yesterday at the barbecue, but he and Forrest didn't interact at all. Considering her pet's reaction to the man a few minutes ago, Annabel wanted to be sure she could pull him away if needed.

Seconds later Smiley was at Forrest's side, instinctively resting his furry head on the man's uninjured leg. Then a deep sigh echoed in the dog's chest.

A full minute passed before Forrest's large hand came to rest behind Smiley's ears, his fingers digging into the dog's thick coat.

Annabel titled her head back slightly and rolled her eyes, upward, pretending a sudden interest in the tiled ceiling. She'd learned it was the fastest way to stop the sharp stinging in her eyes.

Tears, or any sign of pity, were the last thing most people wanted.

The last thing Forrest Traub wanted.

He'd made that very clear while talking to his cousin yesterday about the reason he was in Thunder Canyon for the summer.

"So, Dr. North's secretary seemed a bit hesitant about us being in here." Annabel wanted to talk to Forrest about Smiley being a part of his upcoming medical treatment, but she couldn't just jump into the topic. Not when she'd taken it upon herself to be here instead of waiting for an invitation. "Me and Smiley, that is. Don't tell me your doctor is a stodgy, old curmudgeon who considers his office his inner sanctum?"

"He's not—"

"I'm only asking because the more senior the doctor the more they tend to think the only good medicine is the kind that comes in a pill or from the sharp end of a scalpel." She glanced around for clues, but wasn't close enough to see the graduation dates on the medical degrees hanging from the wall. "Wow, look at all those awards and certificates. Pretty impressive. Then again, this place could use some brightening, a splash of color. Everything in here is brown."

"Annabel—"

"No family photos on his desk. There's not even a plant," she pushed on, afraid if she shut up Forrest was going to kick her and her dog out. "His secretary practically has a jungle around her desk. You'd think she'd put at least one green leafy thing in her boss's office."

"Annabel, stop."

Forrest's soft, yet firm command included an unspoken request for her to look at him. She obeyed, while holding her breath.

"I know why you're here," he said.

She waited a moment, then air became a necessity. "You do?"

"I know all about the work you and your dog do."

"Smiley."

"Excuse me?"

"My dog's name is Smiley, and how do you know?"

"Your sister is very proud of you...and Smiley." Forrest looked down at the dog, continuing to scratch him behind his floppy ears. "But I don't think he can help me."

Annabel had heard those words, many times before and from many different types of people. Young children fighting diseases they couldn't pronounce, the elderly fighting to hold on to their memories and their dignity, and those fighting for the most important thing of all, hope.

"How do you feel?" she asked. "I mean, right now?"

Forrest shook his head. "Forget it, Annabel. I'm not going there."

"I'm not trying to psychoanalyze you." She moved closer. "And I know there's nothing medically we can do—"

"Good. That's my job."

Annabel whirled around at the very deep, very male voice coming from the open doorway.

She immediately cataloged a pair of men's shiny black shoes, dark slacks with a sharp crease down the center of each leg, a cobalt-blue shirt, striped tie and white lab coat.

Dr. Thomas North.

Before her perusal could get past a nicely chiseled jaw, Smiley bounced across the office, pulling his leash to its full length.

Offering an enthusiastic greeting that included a playful bark, her pet rose on his back legs and planted his front paws on the man's midsection.

The move knocked the doctor back against the door frame and sent the paperwork in his hands flying everywhere.

"Smiley!"

Horrified at her pet's unusual behavior, Annabel rushed to help. A quick tug on the collar and Smiley dropped back to all four paws on the ground, but the tail continued to wag up a storm.

"I'm so sorry!" She quickly wound the dog's lead around her palm, pulling him back to her side. "He usually doesn't act like this. I have no idea—" She then focused on the mess on the floor. "Oh, here, let me help you!"

Dropping to her knees, she started grabbing the loose pages and the manila folders, but the man in front of her mirrored her actions. Their heads collided with a resounding crack.

"Oh, fudge nuggets!" Annabel swore and fell backward, landing on her butt. She rubbed hard at the stinging at her temple hoping to erase the pain.

Darn, that hurt!

Suddenly, the warmth and strength of male hands, one capturing her rubbing fingers and the other cupping her jaw, caused a shiver to dance over her skin.

"Look at me. Are you all right?"

Annabel blinked hard as her world tilted. She could swear she saw a dizzying array of stars.

Forcing her gaze upward, she found icy blue eyes, serious and probing and perfectly matching his shirt, staring intently back at her.

Forget the stars.

This was a full-blown meteor shower.

Thomas North knelt on the carpet, cringing at the wrinkled paperwork beneath his feet.

The last thing he'd expected when he hurried into his office, cursing himself for being late thanks to his weekly breakfast date with his grandmother, was to be attacked by an overgrown hairy beast.

Or by the woman who was obviously its owner.

"Hello, miss? Did you hear me? Are you okay?"

"Y-yes, I think so."

Ignoring how her breathy words warmed the inside of his wrist, then transformed into a tremor that raced up his entire arm, Thomas focused on her pale blue eyes. They seemed clear and bright, but her speech was a bit slow.

He waved his hand, holding up three fingers in front of the woman's face. "How many fingers do you see?"

"Two."

Hmm, not good.

His own head still smarted from where they'd

come together with a hard *thunk,* but he didn't have any problem directing Forrest Traub back into the chair he started to rise from or to see the beautiful blonde on the floor in front of him.

Not to mention another blond, with four legs and a wet nose, who was getting in his way.

"And a thumb."

"Excuse me?"

"You're holding up two fingers, index and middle, and your thumb." She laid a hand on the dog's snout, where it tunneled into her loose waves at her shoulder. "I'm okay, Smiley. Please, sit."

The dog obeyed the woman's command, just barely, as its backside continued to shimmy, helped by the rapid wagging of its tail.

Thomas took the paperwork from the woman's grip, added it to the pile he'd shoved back into the top folder. He handed it all to his secretary, who stood over his right shoulder. "Can you put this back into some semblance of order, please?"

"Wow, how did you know she was standing there?" the woman asked, drawing his attention back to her.

"He's got eyes in the back of his head," his secretary quipped as she stepped around them and headed for his desk. "It's something they must teach them in medical school."

Thomas did what he always did when Marge got mouthy. Ignored her. She'd come with the office, having worked for his predecessor for a dozen years, and knew the inner workings of the hospital like the back of her hand. Thomas had only been at TC General two years and he'd be lost without her.

Concentrating on getting the woman back on her feet, he rose and held out one hand. "Do you think you can stand?"

"Of course I can."

She grabbed his wrist with a surprisingly strong grip, and pushed to her feet. He couldn't help but notice the dark polish on her bare toes, the snug fit of her jeans over curvy hips or how the loose ruffled neckline of her blouse had slipped to reveal one bare shoulder.

"Annabel, are you sure you're okay?" Forrest asked.

She turned her head, sending long waves of blond hair flying, covering that shoulder. "Yes, I'm fine."

Thomas swallowed hard and pulled from her heated touch, refocusing his attention on his patient and the reason he was here.

"I don't mind your girlfriend being at your appointment, Mr. Traub—" he moved to sit at his desk, not surprised to find Marge had already left the office, closing the door behind her "—but a dog is a different matter entirely."

"She's not my—"

"Oh, I'm not his girlfriend." The woman dropped

into the second empty chair. "Forrest and I are practically family. I'm Annabel Cates."

Thomas tucked away the news these two weren't involved, and why he even cared, to concentrate on finding out what exactly was going on. "Then what are you and your dog doing in my office, Miss Cates?"

"Two reasons, moral support and a proposition you can't refuse."

Chapter Two

"Oh, and please call me Annabel. This is Smiley."

Thomas watched the oversize furball move to sit between her and his patient, ears flopping as it looked back and forth between the two. Then the mutt leaned toward Forrest. Thomas was about to call out, until he saw how the dog rested its chin lightly on Traub's uninjured knee.

"Smiley is a certified therapy dog," she continued. "As his owner and handler, I've been trained and certified, as well. Because of Forrest's injury, and his ongoing treatment, I thought Smiley might be able to help."

He looked back to the woman. "Help how?"

"Therapy dogs are used to assist patients in dealing with the stress and uncertainty that comes with medical issues."

Thomas didn't put much stock in therapy dogs—or meditation, or aromatherapy, or any number of other alternative therapies that floated around out there.

All he believed in were cold, hard facts. And science.

"Miss Cates, I really don't have time for this. Your visit today is not authorized, by me or, I'm guessing, Mr. Traub, and is distracting to say the least."

"Oh, I don't mean to be any trouble—"

"You've already been that." Thomas dropped his hand to the folder in the middle of his desk, drumming his thumb repeatedly on the cover. An action her dog apparently took as a cue to perch its large front paws on the edge of his desk and swat its large, fluffy tail at the shoulder of Forrest Traub.

"Smiley, stop that and get down." She gently tugged at her dog's leash. "I'm so sorry, Dr. North. I promise you he never acts this way. I guess he must really like you."

"I doubt that."

The dog sat again and returned its attention to Forrest. Miss Cates did the same. "I guess this wasn't such a good idea. Maybe you can spend time with Smiley another day."

"I'd like you to stay." Traub laid his hand back on the dog's head. "Both of you."

Surprised by his patient's request, Thomas studied him closely, silently admitting the animal did seem to be having an impact on the man.

He and Forrest had only met twice before, the last time being a week ago when Thomas had performed a thorough examination of the ex-soldier's injured leg. Forrest had been withdrawn and testy, speaking only when asked a direct question.

In the subsequent reading of his military medical records, Thomas had found the former army sergeant had good reason for his surliness, having gone through hell after a roadside explosive destroyed the Humvee he was riding in during his last tour in Afghanistan.

He'd been in and out of hospitals for the past year and still had not regained full use of his leg. Today though, he seemed more relaxed, a hint of a smile on his face as he continued to scratch the animal's ears and neck.

Of course, this had to be temporary. Depression was common in veterans, as was post-traumatic stress, and Thomas couldn't see how patting a dog could counteract such difficult conditions. The only real cure for Forrest was in the skilled hands of a surgeon.

At any rate, the man clearly enjoyed the dog's

company, so Thomas had no choice but to let the mongrel—and Miss Cates—stay.

"Fine." Thomas flipped open the folder. "We planned to discuss my findings and go over recommendations for further treatment. Are you comfortable discussing your condition in front of Miss Cates?"

"Don't worry about me. I've been present at doctor-patient consults before. Confidentiality isn't an issue," the blonde spitfire said with a wave of her hand. "I know how to keep a secret."

Thomas ignored her and waited for his patient to reply.

"Yeah, go ahead," Traub said.

"The results are a bit complex and cover a lot of technical jargon—"

"Get to the bottom line, doc."

Thomas did as requested. "You are going to need surgery. Again."

He waited, but Forrest's only reaction to the news was the fisting of his free hand while the other continued to dig deep into the dog's fur. Thomas glanced at Miss Cates, but her focus was on his ceiling as she blinked rapidly.

"How soon?" Forrest asked.

Thomas looked back at his patient. "The sooner the better. We can schedule you for next week."

The conversation continued for several minutes as Thomas outlined the presurgery preparations, what he planned to accomplish with the delicate procedure and the post-care that would be required.

"Okay, then. I'll see you next week." Forrest finally released his hold on the dog and grabbed his cane. Pushing to his feet, he held out his hand. "I'm betting on you to work your magic, doc."

Thomas rose and returned the man's firm grasp, determined to bring all his skills and knowledge to the operating room, like always. "You can count on it, Forrest."

The man returned Thomas's gaze for a long moment before he released his hand and turned away. "Annabel, I'll walk you to your car if you and Smiley are heading out?"

"That would be great, thanks." Rising, she held out her hand. "Dr. North, it was a pleasure. I would appreciate the opportunity to discuss the possibility of us working together in the future."

Thomas took her hand, the warmth and softness of her skin against his again creating that same zing of awareness he'd felt earlier. "Thank you, but I don't see that happening, Miss Cates."

"I'm sure we can come to a meeting of the minds, not quite as literally as we did this time, I hope." Her full lips twitched and then rose into a playful grin. "Besides, I'm known to be very persuasive when I want something."

For some reason, Thomas believed her. "My schedule is pretty full."

"A half hour." Her fingers tightened around his. "What harm can I do in thirty minutes?"

Thomas cleared throat and released her hand. Seeing her again would be crazy. His mind was already made up. To him, dog therapy was nothing but... fluff. Still, the chance to spend time with this bewitching woman was something he couldn't make himself pass up.

No matter how much his logical side told him it wasn't a good idea.

"Okay, thirty minutes. You can call my secretary to set up a date and time. But be warned, I rarely change my mind."

Once a decision had been made, Thomas stuck by that decision. No matter what. It was something the hospital staff had learned about him in the two years he'd been here.

But agreeing to meet with Miss Cates?

Thomas had seriously reconsidered allowing the meeting to take place many times over the past week.

Thunder Canyon General wasn't a large facility, but thanks to the financial boom that came to town a few years back and the hard work of the hospital administrators—including his grandmother Ernestine North until she finally retired a year ago—the facility lacked for nothing.

Including a thriving gossip grapevine that, until recently, he'd never been a part of. An accomplishment Thomas had worked hard at since accepting his position.

He'd come home to Thunder Canyon determined not to make the same mistake twice. Oh, he knew the staff talked about him. Even after twenty-four months he was still considered the "new" guy around here.

His reputation as a skilled surgeon, and a success rate that was all the more impressive here at TC because of his age, followed him from his previous position at the UCLA Medical Center in Santa Monica.

Thank goodness that was the only thing that had followed.

He also knew some at Thunder Canyon General considered his bedside manner a bit…cold, at least to those who confused emotional involvement with professionalism.

A mistake he wouldn't make again.

But thanks to Annabel Cates and her dog he'd found himself the recipient of even more stares, whispered conversations that ended when he appeared and a few hazing incidents, some subtle and others not so much, starting the day after her visit.

The sweater Marge had worn the other day covered in miniature poodles had been a delicate jab, but the not-so-quiet barking his fellow surgeons and residents engaged in whenever he walked into the doctors' lounge was not.

The old-fashioned glass apothecary jar filled with

dog biscuits and tied with a bright bow he'd found on his desk just the other day had been a nice touch. There'd been no card and Marge hadn't said a word about it. Deciding that leaving it in the break room for someone who actually had a pet would only add more fuel to the fire, he'd tucked the jar into the bottom drawer of his credenza.

All of which had to be the reason why Thomas found Annabel on his mind so much over the past several days. While he could admit, at least to himself, there'd been a spark of attraction, she was definitely not his type.

If he had one.

It'd been a while since he'd dated anyone. The women he'd gone out with in the past, when he found the time or desire, were professionals focused on their careers, much like him.

Of course, his last attempt at a serious relationship had dissolved into such a fiasco he ended up having no choice but to seek another job as far away from Southern California as he could get.

Which meant returning home to Thunder Canyon.

Besides, Annabel seemed…well, a bit flaky, idealistic, pushy. They could not be more opposite. Yet when he reviewed his calendar each morning he'd found himself looking for her name.

It wasn't until after Forrest Traub's surgery two days ago that it appeared with the promised thirty minutes blocked out for Thursday afternoon.

Today.

Annabel—and her dog—should be here any minute.

Not wanting a repeat from last time, Thomas sat behind his desk and tried to edit his latest article for a leading medical journal, but after reading the same paragraph three times he was glad when familiar tapping at the door came.

"Come in," he said, recognizing his secretary's signature knock. "Marge, I'm out of red markers. Could you find me a few more, please?"

"Sorry. I come bearing gifts, but not a red marker in sight."

Thomas looked up and found Annabel Cates standing in his doorway. He immediately noticed she wore her hair pulled back from her face in a ponytail. It made her look younger, though the curves presented in her simple bright yellow top and denim skirt said otherwise. He found himself wondering just how old she was.

He stood, his gaze drawn to her bare legs and toes, thanks to her sandals, this time the nails sporting a matching neon-yellow shade.

Details. Thomas was known for being a man of details, but he realized he'd taken in her entire outfit before he noticed the large, leafy green plant she held in her hands.

And the fact she was alone. No dog in sight.

"Don't tell me my secretary is baby—err, dog sitting."

She smiled and it lit up her entire face. Another detail he remembered from the last time she was in his office.

"Nope, it's just me this time. Disappointed?"

"Not in the least. Please, come in."

She did, closing the door behind her before she walked to his desk and held out the plant. "This is for you. It's a Peace Lily."

"Are we at war?"

"No, but I thought the name was fitting and this place needs a bit of color. Also, they're known for tolerance for low light, dry air and are great indoor air purifiers."

"Well, thank you." Surprised that she went to such lengths to pick out the offering, Thomas took the container, pausing when his fingers brushed over hers. He placed it on the filing cabinet next to his desk. "I can't promise I'll remember to water it."

"I kind of figured you were a busy guy, so I included an aqua globe. See?" She walked around the desk and moved in behind him, pointing out the green shaded globe barely visible among the leaves. Heat radiated off her body and he suddenly felt naked without his lab coat. "You just fill it, turn it upside down and jab it in the dirt. It'll water your plant for two weeks before you need to refill."

"Ah, that's…that's a good idea." Damn, he

sounded like a schoolkid nervous to be talking to the prettiest girl in the class. "Why don't we sit down and get started?"

"Sounds great." Annabel stepped back but instead of taking one of the chairs in front of his desk, she moved to the couch against the wall. Skirting the coffee table, she dropped to one end and patted the spot next to her.

Thomas cleared his throat, but joined her, making sure to keep an empty space between them. Not that it mattered. Annabel simply scooted closer.

He fought against the automatic reaction to lean back and rest his arm against the back of the leather sofa. Instead, he scooted forward and braced his forearms on his knees, his hands clasped together.

"I left Smiley at home because I wanted to be able to talk without any furry distractions." She grabbed a large book from an oversize bag at her feet. "You don't have to feel bad or think you're not an animal person because the two of you didn't hit it off. You just haven't met the right one yet."

His shoulders went stiff. "I never said—"

"Most people love Smiley, which makes him so good at being a therapy dog," she continued, opening the book and laying it flat across her lap. "I started this scrapbook to document our training and all the work we do. There are a number of tests that Smiley had to pass before being certified, such as acceptance of a friendly stranger, walking through a crowd or sitting politely."

Thomas cleared his throat. It then closed up completely when Annabel laughed and reached out, giving his arm a gentle squeeze. "You're a special case."

Her heated touch seemed to sear his skin through the smooth material of his shirt. His fingers tightened against his knuckles until she released him. "Ah, that's good to know."

"Smiley was also tested for basic commands and how he reacted to being around other dogs, children and medical equipment and so on."

"I'm guessing all the animals in this program are required to provide health records?"

"Of course. They have to be tested annually and maintain a good appearance. Grooming is a must." She turned the page and pointed to certificates in both her and her dog's names. "We passed every test with flying colors and have been doing this kind of work for the last six months. I document every visit we make, sometimes with photographs, as we are working toward the American Kennel Club's Therapy Dog title. Smiley's been to schools, group homes, clinics and nursing care facilities. Not to mention a couple areas here at TC General."

Annabel gently brushed her fingertips over the pictures on the next page of a young girl lying in a hospital bed, her head covered in a colorful head scarf and Smiley stretched out beside her. "This is

Isabella. She was the sweetest thing. When we arrived to visit with her she asked me if Smiley was an angel. When I asked why, she said she'd just dreamed that an angel was coming to take her home."

Thomas watched as Annabel paused, pressing her fingertips to her lips, and glanced upward for a moment before she went on. "Her mother told Isabella she was too sick to leave the hospital just yet and the little girl said she wasn't talking about their home. That the angel was taking her to God's house. She died six weeks later, just days after her tenth birthday. That last week Smiley and I were there every day."

He had to ask. "Why do you do that?"

She looked at him, her blue eyes shiny. "Do what?"

"Roll your eyes that way. You did it during the appointment with Forrest when I was discussing his surgery and again just now."

"I wasn't rolling my eyes. Not in the traditional sense."

"Meaning?"

"Meaning I'm not bored or exasperated. You see, I tend to get a bit emotional, especially in some of the situations Smiley and I find ourselves involved with. It's a trick I picked up from another dog handler to stop the tears."

"It works?"

Annabel nodded. "My mom told me that tickling

the roof of my mouth with the tip of my tongue will do the same thing, but I'm usually too busy talking—" She stopped and bit down on her bottom lip. "Well, I guess you've already figured that out."

Yes, he had. What he couldn't figure out was why he liked that about her.

"Should I go on?" she asked.

As if he could tell her not to. "Please do."

Annabel turned the page and his gaze was drawn to the photo of a teenage boy holding himself upright on parallel bars, a prosthetic where his right leg should have been. "This is Marcus Colton. He lost his leg last winter in a snowmobile accident. Like most teenagers, what he did best was give his physical therapists a hard time."

"Let me guess. Smiley changed that?"

"We were at the clinic one day when Marcus was being his usual charming self, demanding no one would get him to make a fool of himself by trying to walk, even though he'd been doing pretty well at his rehab for a month by then."

She pointed to the next picture showing her dog sitting calmly at the opposite end of the bars, Annabel just a few feet away holding his leash. "Smiley allowed Marcus to pet him for a few minutes and then he went and sat there, almost daring Marcus to come to him."

"And he did."

"Not the first visit. Or even the second, but Smiley proved to be every bit as stubborn as Marcus. The boy finally relented and now he's making great progress."

She went on, telling him stories of senior citizens who had no one to visit them but Smiley, of the patients attending their dialysis sessions who welcomed the distraction petting a dog brought and schoolkids finding it easier to practice their reading when their audience was a dog.

With each story came more looks upward, a couple swipes at the tears that made it through and a sexy husky laugh, all of which struck a chord deep in Thomas's gut.

"I'm guessing all of this is to convince me to allow Smiley to work with Forrest during his rehab, if my patient agrees," Thomas said when she finally finished. "But why do I get the feeling you are looking for something else from me?"

"Hmm, now that's a loaded question." She closed her book, a pretty blush on her cheeks. "Yes, working with Forrest was my original plan. I still want to now that he's home from the hospital and ready to start his physical therapy, but what I'd really like is to set up a weekly support group here at the hospital. One that's open to any patient who wants to come, no matter what their illness."

While Thomas still had doubts about her work, he found himself enamored of Annabel's spirit. What surprised him even more was the fact he wanted to see her again.

And not just here at the hospital.

"I'm still not completely convinced, but I'll agree to at least consider your idea."

"Really?" Annabel's smile was wide, her blue eyes sparkling up at him. "That's wonderful!"

"There's just one condition." He could hardly believe the words pouring from his mouth. "You agree to have dinner with me."

Chapter Three

Stunned, Annabel didn't know what to say. Anyone who knew her well would say it was the first time she'd ever been at a loss for words.

Especially after she'd spent the past half hour hogging the conversation with a man who'd put those dreamy and steamy television doctors to shame. Without the standard long white lab coat he'd worn the last time she was here, his purple dress shirt and purple, gray and black striped tie brought out just a hint of lavender in those amazingly blue eyes.

Not to mention what the shirt did for the man's broad shoulders.

He wore his dark hair short, but it stood up in

spiky tufts on top, as if he'd been running his hand through it just before she arrived. The sharp angles of his cheeks and jaw were smooth-shaven despite it being late in the afternoon.

Her breath had just about vanished from her lungs when he'd joined her on the couch, his woodsy cologne teasing her senses. Thank goodness she'd remembered the scrapbook so she had something to do with her hands.

Besides attack the good doctor, that was.

"Annabel? Did you hear me?"

She blinked, realized she'd been staring. "You want to go out?"

"Yes."

Considering how hard she'd tried not to sound like a sap with her endless chatter about the therapy dog program, Annabel now found it hard to put her thoughts into words. "With me?"

"Yes, with you. We can talk more about your program. Unless there's a reason why you can't?"

Was "too stunned to reply" an acceptable answer?

"Do you have a boyfriend?" His expression turned serious again. "I didn't see a ring on your finger, but I don't want to presume you are free—"

"No." She cut him off. He'd actually looked to see if she wore a ring? "I'm free, totally free. Free as a bird."

"Is that a yes, then?"

She nodded. "Yes, dinner sounds great."

"Tomorrow night okay?"

Something to do on a Friday that didn't include her dog or a sibling? Tomorrow night would be perfect. "I work until six, but after that I'm all yours."

Thomas cleared his throat and stood, rising to his feet in one smooth motion. "Where do you work?"

"At the Thunder Canyon Public Library." Annabel mirrored his actions, grabbing her bag and slipping it over one shoulder. "I'm the librarian in charge of the children's area."

He waved a hand at her scrapbook. "So, all the work you do with therapy dogs is strictly volunteer?"

"Oh, yes. I don't get paid for any of my visits, other than Smiley sometimes getting a doggy treat or two." She hugged her book to her chest, peeking up at him through her lashes. "But I love the work. The therapy program is one of my many passions, along with books and my family. I guess I'm just a passionate person by nature."

His eyes deepened to a dark blue as their focus shifted to her mouth. A slight tilt of his head, a restrained shift in his body that brought him just a hint closer.

Her tongue darted out to lick her suddenly dry lips. She couldn't help it. Not that she dared think he might—

Yes, she had thought about the man, probably too much, over the past two weeks. She'd been looking forward to this meeting for more reasons than convincing Thomas to allow a therapy group here at the hospital. One she would be in charge of.

Annabel could admit, at least to herself, she'd wanted to find out if the quivering sensations she'd experienced when they'd first met had been all in her head.

They weren't.

"I know a great Italian bistro, Antonio's, over in Bozeman. Where should I pick you up?"

She blinked again, breaking the spell the doctor seemed to weave around her. Antonio's? A dinner there cost more than she made in a week. "Oh, we don't have to go that far. Any place in town would be fine by me."

"My treat, so I get to pick the place."

His tone was persuasively charming, so Annabel simply rattled off her address. And her cell phone number. "You know, just in case."

Thomas nodded, then gestured in the direction of the door with one hand, signaling the end of their meeting. "Until tomorrow night, then."

Annabel stepped in front of him, sure she could feel the heat of his gaze on her backside as he followed her. She turned when she reached the door, but found those blue eyes squarely focused on her face.

"I'll pick you up around seven?" he asked.

She smiled. "I'll be waiting."

She waited.
And waited and waited.

Palming her cell phone, Annabel paced the length of her bedroom, her bare toes scrunching in the soft carpet. Smiley lay at the end of her bed, watching her stride back and forth like he was a spectator at a tennis match.

She'd changed out of the sundress with its matching knitted shrug and into a cropped T-shirt and yoga pants an hour ago, kicking her cute kitten heels back into the bottom of her closet.

After she'd accepted the fact Thomas had stood her up.

She'd really been looking forward to tonight. Yes, the chance to talk more about her idea of a weekly therapy session with Smiley at the hospital was a big draw, but darn it, getting to know Thomas better appealed to her even more.

"It's after nine thirty," Annabel said softly, eyeing the clock on her bedside table. "Why hasn't he called?"

Smiley offered a sympathetic whimper and lowered his head to his paws until a quick knock at her bedroom door grabbed his attention.

Seconds later, her sister popped her head in. "Hey! We're about to start a Mr. Darcy movie marathon now that Dad has gone off to bed. You coming downstairs?"

Annabel gave Jordyn Leigh a forced smile, knowing the "we" she was referring to was herself, their older sister, Jazzy, and their mother, all of whom shared a deep affection for the beloved Jane Austen literary character.

As did she.

"I don't think so," she said. Not even Colin Firth's portrayal of the dashing hero could lift her disappointment—or erase the tiny flicker of hope she still held.

"You know, Mom said she can't believe the three single Cates sisters are all home on a Friday night." Jordyn Leigh nudged the door wider and leaned against the frame. "Of course, you taking a pass on dinner tonight had us all thinking you had other plans."

"I did."

Her sister eyed her outfit. "Dressed like that?"

Annabel sighed and glanced at her phone again. "I decided to change after he didn't show. Almost three hours ago."

"Yikes. Hoping for the old 'if I get into my sweats the jerk will call' effect, huh?"

"He's not a jerk." Her defense of him came easily, even if she had no idea why.

Her sister frowned, but only said, "Why don't *you* call *him?*"

Annabel had thought about it, but the only number she had for Thomas was his office. The last thing she wanted was to leave a pathetic voice mail for him to find first thing Monday morning.

"I don't have his number," she finally said. "He's

got mine, at least I'm assuming he does. I mean, I gave it to him, but—"

"But he didn't write it down or put it in his phone right away?" Jordyn guessed. "So you're thinking he forgot?"

Her number? Their plans? All about her?

Annabel didn't know what to think.

"Well, you know where we'll be if you decide to join us. Mom's insisting we start with the black and white version of *Pride and Prejudice* featuring Sir Laurence, so you have plenty of time before our favorite Mr. Darcy appears."

With that, her sister vanished and Annabel flopped down on her bed, immediately bestowed with a sloppy kiss from Smiley, who'd crawled next to her.

"Oh, buddy, what am I going to do?" She scratched at her dog's ears. "Maybe I should go back to work. Goodness knows I got zero done this afternoon thinking about tonight. Or do I stay up here and drive myself crazy wondering why—"

An odd chiming filled the air. It took a moment before Annabel realized it was coming from her cell phone. Not her usual ringtone that asked a cowboy to take her away.

She sat up and read the display. Caller unknown. Her fingers tightened around her phone. One deep breath and she pressed the answer button. "Hello?"

"Annabel? It's Thomas."

"Oh." She paused. "Hi there."

"I'm sorry. I didn't mean to be a no-show tonight."

She released the air from her lungs, while the ache in her stomach that she'd insisted was due to lack of food eased. "Did you get lost?"

"I never left the hospital." His voice was low and a bit husky. "I was called into an emergency surgery this afternoon and didn't have time to try to get ahold of you. I didn't expect it to take this long, but there were complications."

Stuck at work. She'd never even considered that. "Was the surgery a success?"

"Yes, it was." He sounded surprised. "Thanks for asking."

"Are you still at the hospital?"

"Sitting in the men's locker room. I called as soon as I got out of the shower."

Trying not to picture Thomas standing in front of a locker dripping wet and wearing nothing but a towel was as impossible as stopping Smiley from hogging the bed at night.

So she didn't even try.

"You must be exhausted," she said. "I can hear it in your voice."

"I am, but it's a good fatigue, sort of like a runner's high after completing a marathon. I feel like I could run ten miles." He sighed. "Not really, but that's the only comparison I can think of."

An idea popped into Annabel's head, so crazy it

just might work. "So, I'm guessing you didn't have a chance to eat dinner either?"

"I'll probably grab a burger at a drive-thru on my way home—wait, did you say 'either'?"

"How about meeting me at The Hitching Post? Say in about twenty minutes?"

"The what?"

"The Hitching Post. It's on Main Street in Old Town. You know the place, right?"

Silence filled the air. Annabel crossed her fingers. On both hands.

"Ah, yeah… I mean, yes," Thomas finally said. "I know where it is."

Annabel jumped up and began rifling through her closet. "Great! I'll see you there!"

Thomas slowed his silver BMW to a full stop at the curb, surprised to find an empty parking space so close to The Hitching Post on a Friday night.

He'd never been here before, but he'd heard his coworkers rave about the local hangout. Once owned by a lady with a questionable past, the place was now a restaurant and bar, a modern-day saloon right in the middle of Thunder Canyon's Old Town, an area that proudly retained its Western heritage.

A section of town Thomas rarely spent time in. Then again, he rarely spent time anywhere other than his condo or the hospital.

Stepping out of his car, he thumbed the button

to lock the doors and set the alarm, then headed for the sidewalk.

He hated to admit it, but his plan had been to take Annabel someplace outside of Thunder Canyon where the walls didn't have ears and the gossip didn't travel at the speed of light.

Things at the hospital were finally quieting down, but to be seen together here tonight... Who knew what kind of rumors would fly?

Asking her out in the first place had been crazy enough. Agreeing to meet her here? That he blamed squarely on the fact she'd surprised him by not being angry at being stood up.

And the fact he wanted to see her again as soon as possible.

He started for the front door then realized the place was completely dark.

Geez, how late was it?

He glanced at his watch and then noticed the sign stuck in the front window. Closed for Renovation. What the heck was going on—

"Hey there!"

He turned and found Annabel standing on the corner, cradling two large paper bags in her arms. She was dressed casually in jeans and a distressed leather jacket, her hair in loose golden waves.

Thomas again felt that familiar zing at the sight of her. "Hey, yourself. Looks like this place is shut down."

"Oh, I knew it was closed. At least temporarily. My uncle Frank and my cousin Matt have been overseeing the renovation for Jason Traub and his new wife, Joss, who are the new owners. I only named it as a meeting place."

Meeting place for what? He must be more tired that he thought. "What's with the paper sacks?"

"Dinner!" Annabel beamed. "A care package chock-full of ribs, chicken and steak fries from DJ's Rib Shack. Come on, I've got the perfect place for us to eat."

He joined her, not knowing what smelled better, the food or that sexy floral scent he'd noticed the first time they met.

"Here, let me take those," he offered.

Annabel handed over one of her parcels. The heat from the cooked food warmed his hands. They headed up the street and Thomas was curious as to where they were going. His first thought had been her place, but she'd given him an address that was on the southeast side of town.

At the end of the next block she crossed the street and walked toward a large two-story stone building.

"The Thunder Canyon Library?" He read the sign as they walked past the front steps. "We're eating here?"

"My second favorite place in town."

"Pardon my ignorance, but isn't it closed, too?"

"Don't worry. I have a key." Annabel smiled and

led him around the corner to a tall wooden fence. He followed her directions to open the gate. "Latch that behind us, okay?"

Thomas did as she asked and they entered a shadowed courtyard. Thanks to a full moon, he could see a grassy area to one side with trees and benches and a wooden jungle gym on the other. Straight ahead was a wall of glass doors covered with blinds.

"This is the back way into the children's section. Don't worry, a security light should come on—" A bright spotlight shined down on them, illuminating the area. "And there it is. Come on, this way."

Annabel punched a code into a hidden keypad and pushed open the closest door. She held the blinds to one side and Thomas followed her, watching as she then did the same thing with another keypad on an inside wall. "The outside light will go off in a few minutes."

"Are you sure it's okay for us to be here?"

"What's the matter, doc?" She turned, that same saucy smile on her face. "Haven't you ever broken a few rules?"

Yeah, an unwritten one about dating a coworker's ex-wife.

Not good, especially when he found out the lady hadn't yet told her husband she'd filed for divorce. The fact that the man had been a senior surgeon while Thomas was fresh out of his residency only added to the mess.

"It's not something I make a habit of."

"Well, you're not doing it now, either. This is my domain, remember? I'm allowed to be here anytime I want and I often work after hours." Annabel hit a light switch, bathing the large room in a soft glow. "Ah, almost like candlelight. No need to go with all the lights just for dinner."

It wasn't the intimate setting like a private corner booth at Antonio's, but Thomas had to admit it was close.

"This used to be a storage area before I took it over three years ago," Annabel continued. "I had the place completely gutted and rebuilt from the ground up, including the wall of glass to the outside area. Now the kids have a place to come where they don't have to be quiet like upstairs. Well, not as quiet."

Thomas looked around, taking in the floor-to-ceiling bookcases, the scattered tables and chairs, most sized for patrons under four feet tall, as well as several large pillows, comfy armchairs and knit rugs covered hardwood floors.

Posters of children's authors and book covers decorated the walls. A curved wooden desk that must be original to the building stood against one wall, and above it hung a framed headshot of a grinning golden retriever that had to be Annabel's dog, with a placard that read Honorary Mascot.

"Come on, grab a piece of floor."

He turned to find Annabel kneeling at a child-size

table, removing a couple of water bottles from the paper bag. She paused to peel off her jacket, revealing a faded Johnny Cash 1967 concert T-shirt that hugged her curves in all the right places.

Thomas had to swallow the lump in his throat before he asked, "You plan on eating right here?"

"Of course." She pushed aside a couple of miniature chairs and grabbed two large character-decorated pillows. "Here, you can have Dr. Seuss, in honor of your profession. I'll take Winnie-the-Pooh."

Shaking his head, he joined her on the carpet, their hips bumping as they worked to empty the bags of their dinner. Thomas edged away, determined to keep this night light and easy. "So, how did you become a librarian?"

"Freshman-year biology."

That got his attention. "Excuse me?"

Annabel opened one of the containers and the spicy tang of barbecue filled the air. "As a kid I was always the one bringing home stray cats or injured birds. I even stole a horse from a rancher who was using inhumane training techniques on the poor animal. My family thought I'd grow up to be a veterinarian or maybe even a doctor. But when I got to high school and was told I had to dissect a defenseless little frog…" Her voice trailed off as she shuddered. "I just couldn't do it."

Thomas grinned. "You do know the frog was already dead, right?"

"Yes, I knew that, but I still didn't understand why we couldn't learn what we needed without killing…cutting—anyway, I organized a protest which pretty much ended my science career. So I got my bachelor's degree in English from San Jose State University, stayed on to get my master's in Library Sciences and here I am."

He was surprised to hear she'd gone to school out of state. "You went to college in California?"

"With the size of my family a full scholarship made it an easy decision." Annabel filled two plates with ribs, chicken and fries. "I loved it. The bay area is so beautiful."

"And yet you came back here afterward?"

"Of course, Thunder Canyon is my home." She pushed a plate in his direction. "This smells heavenly! Let's eat!"

It was a far cry from the refined dinner he'd originally envisioned, but the food was terrific. They ate picnic style with Thomas trying his best to work with the plastic silverware and keep his meal out of his lap.

"You know, messy is the only way to go." Annabel took a barbecued chicken leg in her fingers and attacked it with a large bite. "Mmm, so good."

Thomas smiled. Her lack of pretense impressed him. Most of the women he'd dated seemed to refrain from eating altogether. Annabel approached her meal the same way she approached the rest of her life—with gusto.

Messy gusto.

"And you do know the caveman method to dining will always result in more sauce on your face and hands than in your mouth, right?" Thomas asked, then smiled even wider at the exaggerated indignation on her face. "You've got a large dollop on your cheek."

His breath caught the moment her tongue snaked out, trying to capture the evidence. It should look comical, but Thomas was captivated. "Ah, other side."

She repeated the motion, but still missed.

"Here, let me help..."

He leaned closer, brushing at the side of her mouth with his thumb the same moment Annabel tried again, and was stunned when the quick lick against his skin sent shock waves through his body.

Her blue eyes widened and he couldn't stop himself from dragging the moist digit over her full bottom lip.

Three dates in the past two years, longer than that since he'd even wanted to feel a woman's mouth beneath his, but right here, right now, there was nothing Thomas wanted more in the world than to kiss Annabel.

And damn the consequences.

Chapter Four

For the second time in two days, Dr. Thomas North had left her utterly speechless. Breathless, too. Heck, the only way Annabel knew she was alive was the hot flush burning across her skin and the way her heart was about to jump out of her chest.

Then again, her heart had been rocking and rolling to its own crazy beat from the moment he'd agreed to her spontaneous dinner invitation earlier tonight.

Less than an hour ago, she'd skidded to a stop in her favorite black ballet flats as he'd eased out of his shiny sports car, looking relaxed despite hours spent in surgery, and especially yummy.

His white dress shirt and khaki pants were still fresh and polished. The only concession to his long day were the shirtsleeves folded halfway to his elbows. Even the loafers on his feet gleamed in the streetlights.

She'd used the few moments it'd taken him to notice The Hitching Post was closed to reassure herself that her idea of a take-out meal at her home away from home was a good idea.

Especially after he'd joined her and she'd seen the deep lines of fatigue bracketing his eyes.

Now, however, those icy blue eyes were bright and alive, the exhaustion replaced with longing as they stayed locked on her mouth. The heavenly back and forth friction of his thumb against her bottom lip had her wondering just how amazing it would be to kiss this man.

Should she or shouldn't she?

Despite her flirty and confident attitude, Annabel had no idea how Thomas would react if she threw caution to the wind, closed the short distance between them and pressed her mouth to his.

The barest taste of him lingering on her tongue from where she'd licked his thumb wasn't nearly enough. She wanted more. Did he? The way he continued to touch her, his fingers brushing her neck—

"I'm sorry." Thomas jerked his hand away. Grabbing a napkin, he thrust it at her while managing to effectively put space between them without moving an inch. "That was— I'm sorry."

"No need to apologize." Annabel wiped her mouth, dropping her gaze to the alphabet-patterned rug. Was he sorry about touching her? Almost kissing her? Not wanting to know, she purposely misunderstood his regret. "Messy eating and barbecue go hand in hand, I guess."

"No, I mean I'm sorry about tonight. This isn't exactly the meal I had planned when I asked you to dinner."

"Plans change." Annabel put the chicken leg back on her plate while offering what she hoped was a casual shrug of one shoulder. "Besides, sometimes the best things happen when we least expect it."

"Maybe so, but I'm the kind of guy who likes to have everything fall neatly into place."

That didn't surprise her. He seemed the type who liked to have every *i* dotted and *t* crossed, as her father often said.

Her?

Not so much. Most of Annabel's life had been a crazy, mixed-up mess of spontaneous opportunities and gut decisions that either worked out better than she hoped or provided a much-needed life lesson.

Hoping for the former, she decided to steer the conversation to a safer topic. "I guess your surgery today didn't go as planned either, huh?"

"No, that was another surprise." He took a long

draw on his water. "What should've been a simple lumbar spinal fusion went totally out of whack when we discovered more damage to the spinal cord than we originally believed. Then the allograft was rejected even though a positive match had been achieved beforehand, resulting in us having to take bone from the patient's pelvis—"

Thomas suddenly stopped speaking, the self-conscious grin on his face making his chiseled cheekbones even more pronounced. "I'm sorry. Again." He braced an arm on a bent knee and waved his hand in the air as if to erase his words. "I tend to get carried away when I talk about work."

The change in him was amazing. He'd grown relaxed and animated at the same time. "Oh, please, tell me more." Annabel tucked her legs to one side. "I think it's fascinating."

He did as she asked, going into great detail about the remarkable work he and his surgical team had accomplished today and the more he talked, the more those amazing dimples appeared. Most of the technical stuff went right over her head, but it was fun to listen anyways.

"I'm guessing you didn't have any problem with slicing and dicing back in high school?" Annabel asked.

Thomas's featured softened. "Never even hesitated."

"So how did you end up here in our little corner of paradise?"

"Thunder Canyon is my home, too."

Now that surprised her. She guessed him to be in his early thirties, which would've put him a few years ahead of her in school, but she found it hard to believe someone as good-looking as Thomas had missed being caught on the radar of her older sisters. "Really?"

"Born and raised. Well, born anyway. I started attending private schools when I was around ten. After that it was summer camps or trips abroad until I went to college at seventeen."

"Considering who I'm talking to, I'm going to assume you skipped a year or two in high school and not the more common late-year birthday?"

"I completed high school, college and med school in nine years. Most people take the standard twelve."

Wow, she was impressed. "So did you follow the family business?"

"No, my parents are lawyers. They have a law firm here in town." He looked away, but not before she saw a muscle jump in his cheek. "They probably expected their only child to follow in their footsteps, but I've known what I wanted to do with my life since I was seven years old."

"That young? I was still undecided between being a princess or the presidency." Annabel read the seriousness in his gaze when he turned back to her. "What happened to create such a deep conviction?"

"My grandfather lost both his legs in a car accident that year." Thomas paused, pressing his lips into a hard line. When he continued his voice held a quiet intensity. "He changed after that. Sank into a deep depression that as a little boy I didn't understand. Even though Grandpa Joe lived almost another twenty years, he was never the same man I knew and loved."

A warm, protective feeling came over her. She blinked hard to erase the stinging in her eyes. "Oh, Thomas."

"I remember telling my parents if I was a doctor I could have saved my grandfather's legs. After that, there wasn't any question about what I planned to do with my life."

"And from what I've heard, you do your job very well."

His gaze flew back to hers. "What you've heard?"

"From you. Tonight. When you talked about that surgery I could tell how much you love your work and how good you are."

"Ah, yeah…thanks." Thomas glanced at his watch. "Wow, look at the time. It's almost midnight."

Okay, she could take a hint. "And you've been at the hospital since before dawn."

One brow arched in inquiry.

"You know what a small town Thunder Canyon

is." Annabel shrugged and started to clear up the remains of their meal. "I've heard your name bantered about. Nothing but good things, of course. Like your tendency to work very long days."

"Yes, well, I've heard a few things about you, too." He joined her, collecting the empty containers. "You and your dog are a popular topic at the hospital."

"It's all Smiley. He makes an impression everywhere he goes."

"How did you two get involved in that line of volunteer work?"

"I had a guest speaker here at the library earlier this year who spoke about the special work dogs do, from assistance for the blind and physically challenged to the therapy dog program. I knew right then my sweet little bundle of fur would be great at it."

"That dog isn't so little."

Annabel laughed and headed for her desk. She was glad they were talking about Smiley. Until now she hadn't even thought about her plan to use this time to persuade Thomas to give the go-ahead for her idea. "But he is sweet, gentle and kind. He also instinctively knows when someone is in pain or needs a good dose of unconditional love."

"What my patients *need* is excellent health care, which comes from scientifically proven methods and top-of-the-line medicines."

"I agree." She ducked behind her desk and, hidden from his view for the moment, stuck out her tongue at his lofty tone. Not mature, but it felt good just the same. "But sometimes they need someone who will listen when they talk and love them without expectations."

"Annabel, I don't want you to think I'm a total jerk—"

"I don't think that." Rising, she found Thomas standing in the middle of the room, his hands shoved deep in his pockets. He should've looked out of place, surrounded by miniature furniture and bright colors, but his serious expression made her want to bring back the relaxed one from earlier. "Not totally. At least not yet."

One side of his mouth rose into a half grin. She'd take it.

"Thanks, I think. I'm just not sure that petting a dog can have much effect on a serious medical condition."

"I don't see how it can hurt."

Hmm, silence from the man. Score one for her and Smiley.

"Okay, I'll give you that," he said.

"How about giving me something more?" Annabel offered a sincere smile as she walked back toward him, shaking out a garage bag. "As in a chance to test your theory? Let Smiley and me work with some of your patients, Forrest included, on a trial basis, and we can see how it goes."

"Annabel—"

She pressed her index finger to her lips, the librarian's universal signal for silence. "Just think about it."

It took a lot of willpower, but Annabel allowed her request to hang in the air as they worked together to fill the bag with their trash and headed for the exit. She reset the alarm, locked the door behind them and pointed out the Dumpster on the far side of the building.

Once they were back on the sidewalk, a cool breeze sent a shiver though her. She started to pull on her jacket, but Thomas gently took it from her.

"Here, let me help."

Turning her back to him, Annabel smiled as she slid her arms into the sleeves, enjoying the gentlemanly gesture.

Tugging her hair free, she peered backward at him. "Thanks."

"My pleasure." The weight of his hands rested a moment at her shoulders then they were gone.

As they headed back toward Main Street to their parked cars, Annabel knew this was the end of their evening, and she wanted so much to ask again about the therapy group. But she'd told him to think about it, and pressuring him wasn't giving him time to think. Still she had to capture her bottom lip between her teeth to stop the words from blurting out of her mouth.

Of course, that move only made her think back to the almost kiss.

Would Thomas want to brush his lips across hers as he said good-night? How would he react if she kissed him instead?

"Which car is yours?"

Thomas's question surprised her and she stopped short. They were back in front of The Hitching Post, but on the other side of the street.

Well, she guessed the saying good-night part was already here.

Annabel pointed toward her vehicle. "The little green Bug. Straight ahead."

Thomas headed toward it and Annabel hurried to catch up with him. "Oh, I'm fine. You don't have to—"

"Annabel, don't argue." He motioned for her to continue moving. "Just walk."

She did, digging her keys out of the bottom of her purse. Hitting the button to unlock the driver's side door, she reached for the handle only to have Thomas's hand shoot past hers first.

He opened her door and she stepped off the curb into the space between the door and the driver's seat. Thomas moved in behind her, his close proximity distracting her for a moment.

Should she turn around? If so, would he still be standing on the curb making him appear even taller?

Darn, why hadn't she slipped on her wedged sandals instead? They would've put her at the perfect height to lean forward, balance herself by lightly placing her hands on his chest before she'd lay a quick kiss on his—

"It'll probably take me a few days to secure a room for your group. How about you start two weeks from today?"

She spun around, his words setting off tiny bursts of sparkling happiness—almost as sweet as the kiss she'd been imagining a second ago—that reached all the way to her toes. "Oh, Thomas! Really?"

He stood, one hand braced on the door and the other on the roof of her car looking down at her with a smile that turned those miniature fireworks into a full-blown explosion. "Yes, really."

Kiss him!

Fighting off the internal command to throw her arms around his neck took all of Annabel's strength. She clasped her hands together and held them tight to her chest, just in case.

He took a step backward, his hand coming off the roof. "My secretary will call you with the details. We'll put the word out about your group, but I can't guarantee anyone will agree to come. Or how many sessions you'll have. That all depends on the patients' reactions and your dog's behavior."

Trying to feel grateful he'd saved her from making a fool of herself, again, she concentrated instead on the good news. "I understand. Don't worry. Smiley will be on his best behavior. This is too wonderful for words. I really don't know what to say, but thank you so much!"

"You're welcome."

Deciding to end the evening on an upward note, she dropped into the driver's seat and started the car's engine. She then reached for the door, but Thomas's voice stopped her.

"Thanks for tonight...for dinner."

The pause when he spoke made her look up at him, but he'd moved farther back on the sidewalk, his face in the shadows. "Thanks for meeting me. I had a lot of fun."

He gave her a quick nod in return, then crossed in front of her headlights to his own car on the other side of the street. Pulling out into the road, Annabel stopped at the red light. In her rearview mirror she watched as Thomas made a quick U-turn in the middle of the empty street and headed in the opposite direction, his taillights disappearing into the night.

The light changed to green and Annabel headed for home. As happy as she was about Thomas giving her therapy-group idea a green light, she had to admit his reaction to her reaction did sting a bit.

Had he been able to tell how much she wanted to kiss him?

Heck, he'd started it with wiping the barbecue sauce off the side of her mouth. She'd only been responding to the vibes he'd put out in the cozy setting of the library. Just because she'd been told in the past, by more than a few people, that she tended to leap before she looked, didn't mean she was to blame.

Pulling into the driveway at her family's home, Annabel parked alongside the collection of other cars that belonged to her parents and siblings. She was greeted by a happy, tail-wagging Smiley as soon as she stepped into the darkened kitchen and her victorious feeling returned.

Kneeling, she gave her baby a hug and a treat from his special biscuit jar in celebration. "I did it, sweetie. We're all set for you to work your magic. Provided you follow the rules and do what you're told."

Smiley offered a cheerful bark in return and Annabel hugged him again. So what if her date—if one could even call it that—hadn't ended the way she'd hoped.

"I got what I really wanted tonight," she whispered to herself as much as to Smiley. "That's what counts."

"Hmm, not sure if I like the sound of that."

Annabel's head jerked up at her mother's voice. Evelyn Cates stood in the doorway that led into the family's oversize dining room, flanked by Annabel's sisters.

Jordyn Leigh snapped on the overhead light. "I don't know, Mom, it sounds pretty good to me. So how was Mr. Better-Late-Than-Never?"

"He was fine. I mean, it was fine." Annabel stood. "I told you Thomas got held up in surgery. That's why our plans changed."

"Yet you left and returned with the same sappy grin on your face." Jazzy winked as she headed for the sink with a handful of empty glasses. "And it sounds like you had a better-than-average time on your date, the first one in…what? How long has it been?"

"Refresh my memory." Annabel opened the refrigerator and stuck her head in for no other reason than to escape her sisters' prying eyes. "Which one of us actually had plans tonight?"

"Oh, sis, she's got you there," Jordyn Leigh said, then laughed. "Come on, let's get back to our movie."

"Why do I get the feeling that line 'the lady doth protest too much' fits somehow?" Jazzy shot back. "Hmm, I smell another romance brewing."

"Oh, please. We've already got two bridesmaids dresses hanging in our closet. The last thing we need around here is another wedding."

Annabel jumped at Jordyn Leigh's parting words as her sisters left the room.

Wedding? Who said anything about a wedding?

Grabbing a soda she didn't want, Annabel closed the door. Her mother had stayed behind, her blue eyes filled with the same loving concern she'd shown for all her children over the years.

"Mom…"

"Can I at least ask what it is you got tonight that you're so happy about?"

Annabel explained her plans for Smiley and the therapy group. "This is something I've wanted to do for a long time. Talking about the group and how I want to help Forrest, and anyone else who might come, is the main reason Thomas and I met tonight. I really think Smiley can make a difference."

"I'm sure he will, honey." Her mother smiled. "But I do think your sisters might be right. You haven't been this happy about a date in a long time."

"I'm happy about getting the approval for my therapy group," Annabel said, refusing to allow the memory of the way Thomas had touched her mouth and the desire she'd seen in his eyes come back to life. "Tonight was no big deal. Goodness knows I've had enough missed connections and false starts when it comes to men in the past. I doubt I'll be spending any more time with Dr. North outside of the hospital."

"Okay, dear. If you say so." Her mother leaned in and gave Annabel a quick hug. "I'm going to wash up those dishes before I head to bed. You joining your sisters?"

"No, I think I'll go up to my room. Good night, Mom."

Annabel headed for the stairs, Smiley at her side. She knew her sisters' good-natured teasing was all in fun, and with two recent weddings in their family, Annabel supposed she couldn't blame them for seeing romance where none existed.

She had to admit that Thomas North wasn't anywhere near as stuffy and uptight as she'd first thought. In fact, he was smart, caring and down-right sexy. And if asked, and there was no reason why anyone should, she'd also admit the barest hint of his touch sent zingers to all her girly parts.

However, when he had the chance to kiss her to-night—more than once, in fact—he'd backed off.

So what did any of it mean?

Frustrated, she placed the unopened soda can on her dresser and once again flung herself down on her bed and stared at the ceiling. Was the attraction all in her head?

Or was the hunky doctor very good at keeping his feelings under wraps?

Chapter Five

Thomas pushed the button that activated the garage door as he turned the last corner in the condominium complex. When he moved home two years ago he'd been one of the first people to buy in the gated community and had chosen an end unit in the last row, hoping for as much privacy as possible.

At the time there had only been a couple dozen of the two-story condos in the development. Now there were fifty units along with amenities that included a gym, pool and club house, not that Thomas ever found the time, or the inclination, to use them.

He preferred to take his daily runs in private, usually on the many trails crisscrossing the hills behind the complex or the treadmill in his spare bedroom.

Damn, it felt like forever since he'd done his usual five miles this morning.

After pulling his car inside and shutting down the engine, he locked his BMW and closed the garage door. Heading upstairs, he entered the open living/dining room and went straight to the kitchen.

Tossing his keys next to the pile of mail on the granite countertop, he yanked open the refrigerator and pulled out a cold beer. The cap released with a simple twist and he tilted his head back, downing half the bottle without stopping.

Then he dropped his head back against the wall with a resounding thunk.

Nope, she was still there.

Two more thunks and one empty beer bottle later didn't help.

Annabel Cates, with the most delicious mouth he'd even seen on a woman, was still front and center in his head. Not to mention his other body parts that remembered and appreciated her soft curves, the spicy vanilla scent that clung to her skin and the way she got him to open up and talk about himself as if they'd known each other their entire lives.

He'd even told her about Grandpa Joe.

Tossing the empty bottle in the recycling bin, Thomas grabbed a bottle of water and made his way upstairs, pausing to set the security alarm and turn on a couple of table lamps in the living room. He'd learned the hard way to leave the low lights on all night. The chrome, glass and leather furniture he'd chosen was sleek and modern, but it also hurt like heck when walked into while fumbling around in the dark during those times he needed to leave in a hurry.

He entered his bedroom, stripping as he went. Leaving an uncharacteristic trail of clothing behind him, the last thing he did was put his cell phone, wallet, and the water on the bedside table before crawling naked between the cool sheets.

The clock read 12:35 a.m., meaning he'd been awake for twenty hours, fifteen of them spent at the hospital. He should be exhausted, but closing his eyes didn't help.

All he saw was Annabel.

The way she almost glided when she walked, as if her feet barely touched the ground. The way her lips curved upward in a mischievous grin when she'd asked him about breaking rules. The pride in those amazing pale blue eyes of hers as she showed off where she spent the majority of her waking hours.

Pride that melted into kindness and compassion when he'd revealed how a childhood tragedy shaped his entire life.

Damn, it was going to be a long night.

Thomas groaned, remembering his cell phone needed charging. He plugged it in, took it off vibrate and punched up the volume of his ringtone. Just in case.

His fingers paused when he saw the missed-call

icon. He pressed the code for his voice mail, breathing a sigh of relief it wasn't the hospital when he heard the voice of his buddy in Hawaii who'd left a disjointed message, mixed with the sound of crying babies, that ended with Reid's usual "I hate talking to these damn things" tirade.

Grinning, Thomas pressed the button to return the call, figuring out it was only nine-thirty in the Aloha State. Besides, his roommate through medical school and five years of residency had said Thomas should call because he was spending his Friday night—

"Dr. T!"

Thomas smiled at his friend's greeting. "Dr. Gaines, I presume. It's been a while since I've heard from you."

"Well, you know. The life of a busy doctor."

Yes, Thomas did know about that.

He also knew Reid somehow made time for his beautiful wife, a nurse he met a year after graduating from medical school who'd convinced him to return to her native hometown of Honolulu after they'd married. Now Reid was the father of twin eight-month-old boys who he was constantly sending Thomas pictures of via text messages, and the owner of three prized surfboards.

The former San Diego surfer had found his own slice of paradise.

Wasn't that what Annabel called Thunder Canyon earlier?

Maybe for her. But Thomas often wondered if he would've ever returned to his hometown if not for making the biggest mistake of his life—one that forced him to leave behind everything he'd worked so hard for.

"So it's already Saturday in Montana." Reid's voice filled his ear. "Please tell me you were not at work this late."

"Is that any better than what you're doing tonight?"

"Hey, me and the boys, who finally crashed, thank goodness, are watching my beloved Angels getting their butts handed to them by the freaking Red Sox while the baby mama is out with her posse of girlfriends," Reid shot back. "Hopefully the twins will stay asleep until after she strolls in. Then we'll have some real home-run action going on."

"TMI, buddy." Thomas pushed himself up against the padded headboard, refusing to think about the fact he'd passed up the chance to even get to first base tonight. Twice. "Since Gracie was practically a third roommate back in the day, I already know more about your sex life than I ever wanted."

"At least tell me yours has improved since we last spoke. I think you said something about a lawyer who caught your eye?"

It took Thomas a moment to figure out what his friend was talking about. "Yeah, that was almost a year ago."

"Okay, so it wasn't the last time we talked. Sue me. You still seeing her?"

"No."

"Because..."

"Because our careers kept us too busy." The lie fell so easily from his lips. Thomas grabbed the water and took a long swallow. "Doctor. Lawyer. Long hours all around."

"You are the worst liar I've ever met."

"It once served me well."

His friend sighed. "Dammit, you haven't let go of that yet? It's been almost three years."

This time Thomas knew exactly what his friend was talking about. Reid had had a front-row seat to his stupidity and ultimate humiliation after he'd gotten involved with the wrong woman.

The worst possible woman.

Another man's wife. And to make matters worse he'd actually fallen in love with her.

Except he had no idea at the time she was married, with no plans to change her status.

Not that Thomas had been inexperienced in matters of the heart. He'd dated through high school and college, but most girls wanted more of his time and attention than he was willing to give. His studies had been his main focus, especially during medical school, and that focus switched to his work while living the crazy life of a new doctor knee-deep in his residency.

Then he'd met Veronica, in the parking lot of a hospital function no less, which should've been his first clue. But he'd been riding a high after getting his board certification and acceptance into an orthopedic surgery fellowship right there in Santa Monica.

When the gorgeous redhead thanked him for fixing a flat tire by tossing him the keys to her Aston Martin convertible and insisting they drive up the coast until they ran out of gas, he'd been hooked. By the time he'd returned home after spending the entire weekend in bed at a "friend's" beach house, he'd agreed to keep their romance a secret, which had made it even more thrilling. Of course, he'd thought it was great that she didn't try to monopolize his time and understood his long working hours.

Until it all came crashing down on him less than a year later, when they'd gotten caught by her husband.

Thomas soon found their affair the talk of the medical center and any job prospects there had quietly disappeared despite his outstanding record. Thankfully, his grandmother had pulled enough strings to get him an interview at TC General, for the job he now held.

"Victoria Meadows is history, man." Reid's voice jerked Thomas from his memories. "You got played by a coldhearted witch who used you to make her old man jealous. A man she's still with and who made chief surgeon earlier this summer if I read the news correctly."

Yeah, Thomas had read that, too. "Thanks for the history lesson."

"Look, I know your grand plans of making the staff at UCLA Medical flew out the window after everything came out, but you said you were enjoying your work in Thunder Canyon."

"I am." There was no hesitation in his voice and Thomas realized just how true the words were.

Yes, his grandmother had come through with a job for him, but he'd worked harder than anyone on the staff to earn the position. TC General might operate at a slower pace than UCLA, but the work they did was just as important. "Things are going well here."

"Any pretty nurses on the staff?"

Thomas sighed. "You never give up."

"Hey, buddy, I just want you to be as happy as I am."

Reid's words caused the image of blond wavy hair and blue eyes to slide through his head, fully formed and in color, as if he'd had a photograph of her in his hand.

And just like that he was remembering how drawn he'd been to Annabel's warm smile and infectious nature.

He wanted to be irritated that she kept coming to mind, but he had to admit tonight had been more fun that he'd had in a long time. An improvised experience he usually stayed far away from whenever his set plans changed, but something in Annabel's voice had been hard to say no to when he'd called to apologize for messing up their date.

And later he'd seen the bright burst of desire in her gaze making it clear that if he'd wanted to kiss her she would've welcomed his mouth on hers.

If he'd wanted? Who was he kidding? His hand fisted the sheets as he remembered how it'd taken every ounce of discipline he had not to take things to the next level tonight.

Annabel was unlike any woman he'd ever met, nothing like—

Thomas cut off that thought.

Getting involved with someone who'd be a presence around the hospital was the last thing he wanted. And she would definitely be around, now that he'd actually given the okay to put that crazy idea of hers into action.

A mutt that could make sick people well? Who was he kidding? Wait until the hospital gossip grapevine got a hold of *that*.

Thomas scrubbed at his eyes, his bones aching with exhaustion. Chalking up his reaction to Annabel Cates and her dog therapy plan to being overtired was easy to do.

Maybe sleep would be easy now, as well.

"North, did you pass out on me?" Reid asked. "It got real quiet all of a sudden."

"No, still here, but fading fast. I should go."

"Okay, I'll hang up. Oh, but before you drift off

to dreamland I'm going to text you a picture of the newest member of the family."

Thomas must be more tired than he thought. "What? You and Gracie have another kid I didn't know about?"

"No, we agreed to foster a dog from the local animal rescue center a couple of weeks ago, but she's the sweetest pup and fit so well with the Gaines clan we had to keep her."

"Let me guess." Thomas closed his eyes and again dropped his head, the headboard muffling the sound this time. "A golden retriever?"

Reid chuckled. "How the heck did you know that?"

Over the past few days Thomas swore he'd dreamed about dogs every time he closed his eyes.

Being chased by a Great Dane during his daily run. His take-out lunch scarfed right off his desk by a basset hound with ears so long the animal had tripped on them while making his getaway. Performing a knee replacement on a police K9 unit dog, a German shepherd who'd been hurt in the line of duty. These were just a few of the crazy scenarios that invaded his sleep.

He had no idea what all that meant, but he figured it had something to do with the fact Marge had surprised him on Monday afternoon when she'd announced she'd found a meeting room for Annabel's sessions and that they were ready to start this week.

Or maybe it was because over the weekend Thomas had started to do his own extensive research on the results achieved by dog therapy programs. He told himself it had nothing to do with Annabel and everything to do with his responsibility as a staff member at the hospital to know all he could about a program he'd indirectly offered to his patients.

Yeah, right.

So why had he been standing here in the hall on Wednesday afternoon, watching through the open doorway for the past fifteen minutes while Annabel and her dog worked the crowded room? He really needed to get back to his office.

"Dr. North?"

Thomas turned and found a trio of nurses from his surgical team passing him by in the hallway. "Ladies."

"Hmm, that's a new look for you, Doctor." Michelle, the newest of the three and fresh out of the army, had only been at TC General for a month. "Blue is your color."

One of the other nurses quickly elbowed her and the three hurried away, but not before Thomas saw the smiles on their faces.

Glancing down at the standard blue surgical scrubs he wore, Thomas silently acknowledged they were far from his usual attire of dress slacks, shirt and tie. The outfit, complete with thick-soled sneakers that were perfect for long hours on his feet, was comfortable and familiar. He'd practically lived in scrubs during his residency, but now they were something he was never seen in outside of surgery.

Until today.

Now that he thought about it, he'd gotten more than a few stares and smirks since he'd donned the clothes an hour ago. He'd planned to head to his office to change into the spare suit he kept there, but not until he'd completed his rounds.

Then he'd purposely taken a route that brought him right by this meeting room with the idea of observing Annabel for just a moment—

"Dr. North." This time his name was spoken as a statement, not a question and by a voice that held the familiar rasp of maturity and authority Thomas had known his entire life. "I assume there is a fascinating explanation for your current attire."

He turned back and there stood a wisp of a woman at just over five feet tall with steel-gray hair pulled back into a perfect chignon and the same icy blue eyes as him.

"Hello, Grandmother."

She didn't return his greeting as her chin rose a degree while her gaze traveled the length of him.

Thomas straightened his shoulders and stood a bit taller. Force of habit. Despite celebrating her eightieth birthday a few months ago and, more recently, her retirement from her position as a hospital administrator, Ernestine North was still a force to be reckoned with within the halls of TC General.

"And your choice of foot apparel, as well," she finally said with a hint of a smile. "Please don't keep me in suspense."

"I had a patient who had an…er, adverse reaction to his medication while doing my rounds. This was the only choice for me to change into at the time." Thomas relaxed and crossed his arms over his chest. "And I like your shoes, too."

His grandmother leaned on her cane and lifted a foot, offering him a better display of her red-and-white polka-dot shoe with tiny white bows at the ankle peeking from the hem of her navy blue pantsuit. "Yes, they are adorable, aren't they?"

"And a bit too tall. I thought your doctor said no more high heels."

"I'm old. I don't have to listen to him. Besides, the heel is less than two inches." She set her foot down and waved the cane at him. "I don't really need this. I just use it to make myself look authoritative."

More likely because the cane had once belonged to his grandfather, until he had no use for it after his accident. She'd started using it the day of Joe's funeral and Thomas had never seen her without it since. "You're retired, Gran."

"Yes, but many of the staff still fear me in my honorary position. I like it that way."

"Gran—"

"But we weren't talking about me. Did it ever occur to you to keep an extra suit in your office?"

"Of course." Thomas grinned, enjoying the banter. "I'm headed there right now to change."

"No, what you are doing is standing here. Why?" She glanced around, the double take when she spotted Annabel and her dog was slight, but Thomas saw it. "Ah, the dog whisperer."

"She's not a dog whisperer. Annabel Cates is certified in dog therapy and she's doing a weekly session here at the hospital for anyone, including staff as you can see, who wish to stop by."

His grandmother remained silent, the tilt to her head saying more than any words could.

Damn. Had he actually been defending her?

"Yes, I know who Miss Cates is. I read your memo and wanted to stop by and see how things were going." His grandmother stepped closer to him and out of the way as people started to exit the room. "Apparently, I'm not the only one who thought to do so."

Annabel's sweet laughter spilled from the room and Thomas found it impossible not to look.

She knelt in front of a young girl who couldn't have been more than three years old. The child tried to wrap her arms around the furry neck of Annabel's dog, who sat quietly in front of her, his wagging tail the only part in motion. Annabel laid a hand on the dog's shoulder and he bowed his head. The child completed her hug; the woman behind her who was doing her best to hold back her tears had to be the mother.

Annabel smiled when she accepted a hug, as well. She then turned, as if she'd felt his gaze on her, and sent him a quick wink he felt all the way to his toes.

"Thomas?"

It took more effort than it should, but Thomas gave his attention back to his grandmother, not realizing she'd stepped a few feet away to speak with a hospital volunteer. The woman in the pink smock walked away, but Ernestine stood there, a single arched brow that told him she was waiting for an answer to a question he hadn't heard.

"I'm sorry, Gran. What did you say?"

"You seem different, Thomas. Where is that straitlaced, perfectionist grandson I know and love?"

Thomas fisted his hands for a moment, her words delivering a light blow he didn't like. Because it was a direct hit?

"I am not straitlaced."

"Of course you are. It's a family trait. And I asked if you plan to attend your parents' dinner party tomorrow night."

Her question had him wanting to tighten his grip even more, but he relaxed it instead before his grandmother's sharp gaze spotted his reaction. The woman was already well aware of the distance between him and his parents, thanks to having grown up more away from home than with them, but he'd go to their dinner party because his grandmother wanted him there. "Yes, I'll be there."

"And please—" she paused, her lips pursed as if she was holding back a smile "—at least wear a tie."

Unable to hold back his own grin, Thomas didn't even try. "At the very least."

She nodded once, turned and walked away, her steps graceful as always. He watched as she made it as far as the nurses' station halfway down the hall before getting into an animated conversation with another staff member.

"Oh, I love her shoes."

Annabel's soft voice carried over his shoulder, catching him off guard. For a moment Thomas wondered if he should've left when his grandmother did, but Annabel had already seen him. He probably shouldn't have stopped by at all. Being seen with her would only fuel the gossip.

A quick greeting and then he'd leave.

He faced her, noticing the meeting room was completely empty now. A couple of steps and he crossed the threshold before a slight nudge at his knee, followed by another more insistent bump, had him looking down at the dog at his feet.

"Smiley insisted on coming over to say hello."

Thomas considered the dog's expression and

damn if the mutt didn't look like he was smiling, before shifting his attention to its owner. "Did he now?"

"Well, I wanted to talk to you, too." Annabel's eyes sparkled. "Because I realized, despite that first meeting in your office, you and my best bud here haven't ever been properly introduced."

"Annabel, that's not really necessary—"

"Smiley, I'd like you to meet Dr. Thomas North." Annabel gave a gentle tug on the leash as she spoke to her dog. "He's the one responsible for us being here and having such a great first session. Please say hello."

The golden promptly sat and lifted one paw.

Thomas couldn't hold back his laughter as he bent over, accepting the offering with a quick shake. "It's nice to meet you, Smiley."

As he knelt down before the dog and took its offered paw, he was struck by a realization. He, Dr. North, was on his knee shaking a dog's paw. And enjoying it. Just like he enjoyed the dog's unpredictable owner.

Chapter Six

It was silly, but Annabel had to blink back the sudden sting of tears biting her eyes as Thomas interacted with Smiley.

Happy tears, for sure.

Today had been wonderful with all the people who'd come by to meet her and Smiley at their introductory session, but Thomas stopping by to see them made the day perfect.

She'd been so worried no one would show, but then Madge, Thomas's secretary, had called this morning and told her about the buzz the notices for her sessions were generating.

She and Smiley arrived this afternoon to find a

half-dozen patients waiting and, as the hour passed, even more stopped by. Not everyone stayed for the entire session, but Smiley had made sure everyone got some much-needed attention.

Even a few of the hospital staff had wandered in, out of curiosity or looking for a bit of comfort or stress relief, an aspect of dog therapy Annabel hadn't even considered until today.

"Did things go as well as you expected?" Thomas asked as he straightened. "I only caught the last few minutes of your session."

Annabel grinned, watching from the corner of her eye as Smiley heaved a deep sigh that signaled his contentment before he lowered himself to the floor, paws stretched out over Thomas's shoes. "Things went better than we could've hoped for."

"You know, I was worried it might be depressing, so it surprised me at how uplifting and hopeful the session seemed to be."

"Thanks. I think."

He blushed and Annabel's insides fluttered like a mass of butterflies taking flight. She loved it.

"No, that's not what I meant. I was just concerned—"

"Hey, I was only teasing." She grabbed his arm and gave him a quick squeeze. The heat of his bare skin against her fingers set off those tingles she'd missed over the past five days. "I was worried, too, but today was more like a meet and greet. To give people a chance to get to know Smiley a bit and see if regular sessions are something they might be interested in."

Thomas pulled from her touch and folded his arms, stretching the cotton material of the scrubs tight across his chest. His fingers rubbed at the spot where she'd made contact with him. Was that good or bad?

"Well, it looked like you had all the age groups covered," he said. "Who was that last little girl I saw you with? She wasn't wearing a patient band on her wrist."

"No, her little brother was born two months premature and is still in intensive care. Their parents came by to check on the baby and the mother thought her little girl would enjoy meeting Smiley."

"She certainly seemed to."

"I'm glad they stopped by. Of course, the one person I was really hoping to see today was Forrest Traub. Do you know if he was notified about the session?"

A shadow passed over Thomas's blue eyes. "Yes, I saw him on Monday and mentioned it."

Her excitement deflated a bit. "He didn't want to come?"

"He's left town, Annabel."

Confusion swamped her. "What? Why?"

"Something came up at his family's ranch in Rust Creek Falls and he decided to return home."

"But what about his leg?"

"I've done what I can, for now. He's still healing and he assured me that scheduling private sessions with a local physical therapist is one of his priorities."

Annabel didn't like the seriousness of Thomas's tone. Although she was glad Forrest would continue to work toward his full recovery, she was worried about his mental well-being.

"You're concerned about him."

"Aren't you?"

Thomas sighed and nodded. Knowing he couldn't discuss a patient's care in any detail with her, Annabel didn't ask, but made a mental note to check in with her sister and the rest of the Traub family.

Maybe a road trip would be necessary? Rust Creek Falls was only about three hundred miles or so from Thunder Canyon.

Setting that idea aside for now and turning her thoughts back to all the good things that happened today was easy. At least four of today's visitors had expressed interest in coming back on a regular basis and two of those were veterans who'd recently served in Iraq. She was determined to find a way to make those sessions happen.

"Did Marge mention she reserved this room for me for the rest of the week?" The surprise on his handsome face answered her question. "Oh, I guess not."

"You plan on being here tomorrow and Friday? What about your job at the library?"

"It'll take some creative scheduling, but I'll make sure Smiley's sessions don't interfere." Annabel tightened her grip on the leash when the pet responded to his name and rose to his feet between the two of them.

"Once I get a better idea of who's interested in attending, I'm thinking of having two sessions a week. One will be like today, more casual, where people can stop by and stay as long as they feel they need to. Maybe I'll even invite some of my fellow volunteers to stop by." The ideas flowed as she spoke. "The other session should be more private with a limited number of attendees. It's amazing how people open up and talk when their attention is focused on something else."

"Like petting a dog."

"Exactly." She looked down, realizing she'd been scratching Smiley behind his ears this whole time. "See what I mean?"

"Somehow I don't think you need anyone's help to open up."

Annabel laughed then said, "I do tend to talk a lot. The curse of trying to be heard in large family, I guess."

"Sometimes that's hard to achieve no matter the size of the family."

Intrigued, Annabel wanted to ask him what he

meant, but the busy hospital sounds from the hallway grabbed his attention and he took a step backward. "I should head to my office. I want to get out
of these clothes."

Need any help?

Annabel managed to hold back the words, but
took the moment to enjoy the view of how the loose-
fitting top and pants still managed to show off
Thomas's strong arms. "Oh, I don't know. I think
scrubs look really good on you."

"Ah, thanks." A beeping noise filled the air. He
reached for the pager at his waist. "Sorry, I need to
answer this. Are you two heading out?"

Smiley's tail started wagging vigorously, batting
both their legs.

"That's a yes in Smiley speak," Annabel said.
"We'll get out your way now."

"You're not in the way. Come on, we're both heading in the same direction."

Annabel tightened her grip on the leash as they
exited the room and started down the corridor. The
whispers and stares that followed them were pretty
standard, Smiley always drew his share of attention, but Annabel noticed how Thomas's demeanor
changed with every step.

Gone was the easy banter between them and that
wonderful smile of his. They were stopped twice
by people asking about the sessions and by the time

they reached the elevators, she could almost sense his relief.

"Well, here's where we part ways, Miss Cates," Thomas said, his attention focused on the button to call for the elevator.

Miss Cates?

Surprised by his formal tone, Annabel forced her feet to keep moving. She kept her reply breezy and refused to look back. "Thanks, Dr. North. See you tomorrow."

Annabel slid her sunglasses on, to ward off the bright sunshine in the hospital parking lot and to hide from her sister's sharp gaze.

"Okay, spill," Abby said. "You've been tight-lipped about the handsome doctor since Wednesday night. Have you seen him in the past two days?"

"Yes, I saw *Dr. North* yesterday."

Abby took Smiley's leash from Annabel's hand. "So, how did it go?"

"Oh, so well he's pulled a complete vanishing act today."

"Do tell!"

Darn! Annabel should've known she'd regret confiding in her youngest sister. They'd shared a private chat Wednesday after a family dinner while enjoying a glass of wine on the front porch.

Her emotions had been flying all over the place ever since she'd left the hospital—excited about the sessions, confused by Thomas's behavior—and all it took was a simple "what's wrong" from Abby for everything to come pouring out.

"Well, running into him yesterday wasn't planned." Annabel moved to one side of the sidewalk to let an elderly couple walk by. Smiley followed her, of course, and so did Abby. "We'd finished up our second session, and unlike Wednesday afternoon Thomas hadn't show up at all."

"But you'd said you thought he wouldn't after the way he dismissed you the day before."

"I know." Annabel hated that she'd been right. "Anyway, we were getting ready to leave when one of the nurses stopped by. She told me about a patient up on the second floor who she thought could use a personal visit from Smiley."

"The patient didn't come to the session?"

"Mr. Owens broke his hip and leg in three places and is bedridden. He's also a widower with no children, almost ninety years old and, according to the nurse, as mean as the devil."

Abby smiled. "And you just couldn't resist."

"Of course not. So, Smiley and I used the stairs as his room was at that end of the hall. I could hear loud voices coming from his room while we were still in the stairway. Heck, everyone on the floor probably heard him arguing with his doctor."

"Oh, no."

"Oh, yes. You know me, I didn't even hesitate.

Thinking Smiley could take the edge off any situation I just waltzed in, and there stood Thomas."

Her sister's eyes widened. "What did he say?"

"He ignored me at first. Well, not really ignored." Annabel lowered her voice, her gaze on the large expanse of grass and flower beds that led to a low stone wall. The tables and chairs of the hospital cafeteria's outdoor eating area sat scattered on the other side of the wall where a few people gathered, enjoying the late summer afternoon. "I doubt either of them stopped arguing long enough to even notice I was in the room."

"Until Smiley made his presence known."

"By making a beeline straight for Thomas."

"Smiley has always had a good instinct about people," Abby said, giving the dog a quick smile. "He must like Thomas."

"He does," Annabel agreed. "So do I, but the good doctor made it clear he wasn't happy to see either of us. Even after his patient stopped grousing the moment Smiley walked to his bedside and said hello. Of course, I followed to make sure things went okay. The next thing I knew Thomas had disappeared."

"And today?"

"Are you kidding? The man probably took a sick day just to avoid running into— Oh!"

"Oh what?"

The moment he stepped outside, Annabel's eyes were drawn to his steel-gray dress shirt and solid black tie, a calming beacon among the sea of colorful scrubs.

Thomas walked with sure strides to the far corner of the patio and sat alone at a table shaded by a large tree, never once looking up from the paperwork in his hand.

"That's him, isn't it?"

Annabel turned and found her sister openly staring. "Yes, that's Thomas North, M.D., but hey, don't be shy. Just go ahead and gawk at the guy."

"Well, he certainly is something to gawk at." Abby looked back at her and grinned. "Go talk to him."

"What?"

"You like him, Annabel. You just said so and after the way you gushed about meeting him for the first time, your impromptu date at the library, the way he filled out those scrubs—"

"Hey! I wasn't gushing."

"Yes, you were, and don't even think about blaming it on the wine." Her sister waved a finger at her. "Believe me, if anyone knows how hard it is to get a man's attention, it's me. I had to practically throw myself at Cade before the guy finally noticed me."

What her sister said was true, even though Cade Pritchett had been a friend of the family's for years and was now her sister's very besotted husband. "But you two knew each other a long time before things got romantic last year."

"Which only made it harder to get the man to see me as anything but the youngest of the Cates girls. Take my advice, I know what I'm talking about."

With five sisters, Annabel had heard that line many times before. "Famous last words."

Abby laughed. "Trust me."

Unable to stop herself, Annabel gazed across the lawn. "Just jump into the deep end?"

"With both feet and a big splash." Abby blew her an air kiss and crossed her fingers. "Thanks for letting me borrow Smiley. I'll drop him off at the house later. Good luck!"

Annabel stood on the sidewalk as her sister and Smiley disappeared among the cars in the still-crowded parking lot. Checking her watch, she saw it was almost six and Thomas was still here.

Sitting at a table, alone, with his back to everyone.

Giving a tightening tug on her ponytail, Annabel wished for a cuter outfit than her pink cotton blouse and wrinkled khakis, and headed for the stone path that led to the dining area.

She paused when she reached his table. "Hi there."

Judging from the way his head jerked up, she'd surprised him. He stared at her, but thanks to the dark lenses of his sunglasses, she couldn't read anything in his gaze.

"Am I interrupting?"

He closed the folder. "No, of course not."

Without waiting for an invitation, Annabel

dropped into the chair opposite him and went cannonball style with her opening line. "I'm sorry for my unannounced visit to Mr. Owens's room yesterday. It was wrong of me to bring Smiley to a patient without asking for permission first. It won't happen again."

Thomas sank back into his chair.

Annabel wasn't sure how to take his relaxed posture. The hard line of his mouth didn't help and she wished desperately he'd remove the sunglasses, which probably cost more than her entire outfit, so she could see his eyes.

"It's just that after I heard about his condition and his attitude, I thought—"

"How did you find out about him?"

Why did she think he already knew the answer? "One of your staff mentioned him to me at the end of Smiley's session. I guess because he's a patient of yours, she felt it was okay to recommend a private visit." Annabel then remembered her own sunglasses and shoved them up onto the top of her head. "I didn't know he was your patient until I walked into the room, but still…that's no excuse."

He stared at her, as still as a statue. It was like playing the "who will blink first" game and Thomas didn't know it, but Annabel was the family champion. She'd wait him out if it took all night, but she wasn't leaving until he accepted her apology.

Yanking off his own sunglasses, Thomas rubbed

at his eyes with the back of his hand before tossing the glasses on the table. "Annabel, I—"

"Hey! It's Smiley's mama!"

Annabel jumped when a cool, sticky hand landed on her arm. She turned and found the little girl whose brother was still in the ICU standing there.

"Well, hello to you." She smiled at the girl, loving her twin ponytails of curly blond hair. "Where's your mother?"

"Suzy!"

Annabel spotted the child's mother waving from across the patio. Rising, she shot Thomas a quick look, surprised to see the slight grin on his face. "I'll be right back."

He nodded.

Taking the girl's hand, Annabel walked her back to her mother and visited for a few moments. She wanted to get back to Thomas, to find out what he was going to say to her, but it felt like an eternity passed before she could. Every time she started moving in his direction, she was stopped by people wanting to talk about Smiley and her program.

She glanced over to make sure Thomas hadn't pulled another disappearing act, hoping his attention was at least on his paperwork.

Each time his attention was on her.

She didn't know if that was a good thing or not, but she liked the warmth that spread throughout her, especially when they made eye contact when she was finally able to rejoin him.

"Whew! Sorry about that, but it is nice to know we're making an impact."

"So, where is Smiley?"

His question surprised her. "That's what everyone else asked me. My sister Abby came by to pick him up earlier. She's taking him to hang out at ROOTS."

"Roots?"

"Haven't you ever heard of it? ROOTS is the hangout down on Main Street for local teens. They have all kinds of programs year-round, but the summers are especially busy. Abby works there while she's pursuing her master's degree in psychology."

"Is she a trained volunteer in dog therapy, too?"

"Smiley's not there in an official capacity. He's just hanging out with whoever might be there on a Friday night."

That got Thomas to smile again. "So he can unofficially work his magic? Like he did with my patient?"

Annabel's breath caught in her throat. "He did?"

Thomas leaned forward, his gaze intent as he laced his fingers together over his paperwork. "I owe you an apology, Annabel. Yesterday was a... difficult one, which seems to be the norm for Mr. Owens since his surgery." His gaze dropped away. "I handled your arrival...badly."

The pain in his voice tugged at her heart. She

reached out and laid a hand over his. "He reminds you of your grandfather, doesn't he?"

"Mr. Owens is like many of my elderly patients, obstinate and scared. But today he actually smiled at the nurses and took his medication without issue." Thomas flipped his hand over and captured her fingers in his. "And when I met with him this afternoon he asked when that beautiful girl and her pup were coming back to see him again."

Annabel gasped, surprised at the man's request. "Oh, I'm sorry we didn't get up to see him. Smiley has an appointment at the vet in the morning, but I can come after— Oh, there I go again!"

Thomas's smile widened. "If you can rearrange your schedule I'd appreciate it if you, and Smiley, came back to visit with him again."

"We would love to." Those familiar bursts of tingling happiness that always seemed to happen whenever she was with him filled Annabel's chest. "Thank you, Thomas, and until Mr. Owens is capable of joining us in the regular meeting room, I'll make a point of stopping in to see him afterward. As long as his doctor approves."

"I do, and thank you."

Annabel gave his hand a squeeze and went to pull away, but he held tight.

"You know, I do believe I owe you a dinner out." Thomas leaned closer. "Are you free tomorrow night?"

Oh, those bursts exploded into a dizzying array of bright colors. It was like last month's Fourth of July was repeating itself all over again. "Yes, I'm free."

"How about we try out the Gallatin Room at the Thunder Canyon Resort?"

"Oh, Thomas, that place is so fancy."

"So, let's get fancy. What do you say?"

Chapter Seven

"Dinner reservation for North."

The Gallatin Room maître d' looked up from his station, then smiled. "Ah, Dr. North. It's good to see you again."

"It's good to see you, too, Robert."

"Your table is ready, if you and your companion will follow me."

Thomas placed a hand at the small of Annabel's back, gently guiding her ahead of him as they walked deeper into the restaurant, enjoying the heat of her skin almost as much as the way she jumped at his touch.

The first time it happened she included a breathless gasp that matched his own when he'd gotten his first look at the wide expanse of skin shown by the open back of her clingy black dress. The lacy shawl she'd casually thrown over her bare shoulders and sexy black heels completed the picture.

Thomas had wanted to stop right there in her family's crowded driveway and kiss her until they were both out of breath.

The hell with the fact her parents and two sisters were probably spying on them from inside the house.

Thomas hadn't picked up a date at her parents' home since his senior prom. And according to Annabel, there were still two more sisters, their husbands and a lone brother that he hadn't met yet!

Well, that wasn't exactly true, but for the moment, for this evening, it was just him and Annabel.

As they walked past tables covered in fine white linen, candlelight and crystal centerpieces of red roses, Thomas acknowledged a few friends of his parents and fellow staff from the hospital, with a quick nod.

He didn't know if the slight kick to his gut was from being seen in the company of a beautiful woman or the fact he'd actually asked Annabel out for another date.

And that she so readily accepted.

Somewhere between the gossip and witnessing the positive effect she was having at the hospital in just a few days, Thomas found himself wanting to spend time with her and damn the consequences. A feeling he hadn't experienced in a long time.

His sudden invite had surprised him as much as it did Annabel. Impulsive decisions had never been his strong suit. Thanks to his scientific mind, he tended to think long and hard about everything, but the moment the words had left his mouth yesterday he knew he wanted tonight to happen.

"Here we are, sir." The maître d' stood to one side at the opening to a private area just off the main room, separated by a slight stairway. "The wine you requested has been laid out for you. Your server will be with you shortly."

"Thank you, Robert."

The man's slight nod told Thomas all of his plans were in place, which didn't surprise him. The Gallatin Room was a five-star eatery and one of the finest dining establishments in the entire state of Montana.

He entered the space behind Annabel in time to hear her gasp again as she stood before the floor-to-ceiling windows that looked out over the entire mountain.

"Oh, Thomas! This is glorious!"

He smiled and walked past the perfectly set table for two and joined her at the curved wall of windows. "Have you never been here before?"

She turned to face him, her hair gliding slowly across her shoulders. "Once or twice for a special occasion, but never in this spot and never with this view." Her gaze moved to the table. "Never this fancy."

"Didn't we agree *fancy* is the chosen word for tonight?" Thomas teased, pulling out the closest chair and waiting until she sat before he moved to the other side of the table.

"I think you and I have different definitions of the word." Annabel accepted the glass of wine he poured for her.

"Maybe so," Thomas said, raising his glass in a toast to her. "So I'll go with another word, *beautiful*. You look very beautiful tonight, Annabel."

Pleasure flashed in her eyes, but before she could respond their server appeared with the first course of their meal. Thomas enjoyed Annabel's confusion as a colorful salad plate was placed before her.

Once they were alone again, he reached for his own fork and dug in, but paused when he noticed Annabel hadn't moved. "What is it? Is something wrong?"

"Ah, no." She opened her cloth napkin and laid it across her lap. "Is that a Caesar salad you're having?"

"Yes, it is."

She looked at her plate again. "Mine's a garden salad without the shredded cheese, croutons or onions."

Thomas fought to keep his features passive. "I can see that."

"And the ranch dressing is served in a separate

dish on the side," Annabel persisted, "because there's nothing worse than soggy lettuce."

"That's an interesting reason."

"Thomas, this is exactly the way I like my salads." She leaned forward, her voice a low whisper. "What's going on?"

"Just eat," he replied, matching her tone.

"Thomas—"

He waved his salad-laden fork at her. "I heard your visit with Mr. Owens went well today."

"Yes, it did." Annabel reached for her fork. "He told me the most amazing stories about serving in the navy during the Second World War and how he met his wife in San Francisco after the war ended. Did you know she was a nurse?"

Thomas nodded around a mouthful of food, waiting until he swallowed to speak. "Yes, he mentioned you pointed out how she would expect him to be a better patient."

Annabel laughed. "I did no such thing. He's the one who made that admission. When he told me they'd shared over fifty years of marriage together I agreed that she must've known him better than anyone else in the world."

"Well, I would think so."

"Did you know they fell in love and married within a month of meeting each other?" Annabel paused to take another sip of wine, then sighed. "He told me he knew she was the one for him after their first date. Do you think it's really possible to be so sure that you want to spend your life with someone that quickly?"

"I don't know. My grandparents were married for fifty-five years, after they dated for four years first. Of course, that was because my grandfather was a freshman in college when they met and my grandmother wasn't even out of high school yet."

"My folks have been together for over thirty years. Let's hope long marriages run in the family, huh?"

Thomas's mouthful of salad lodged in his throat.

He coughed and reached for his wine, thankful that Annabel didn't notice his distress due to the amazing sunset outside that grabbed her attention.

"Are you okay?"

Okay, so she did notice. "Yeah—ah, yes, I'm fine."

They finished eating just as the server returned. The empty plates were whisked away and moments later, the main course was served with a flourish.

Annabel's eyes widened as she stared at the offering in front of her. "Surf and Turf?"

"North Atlantic lobster tail with porcini-rubbed filet mignon and apricot-glazed green beans." Thomas provided the specifics as the server silently disappeared again. "Hope it tastes as good as it looks."

"I've only had lobster and steak together a few

times, but I've always considered this combination my favorite meal in the world."

"Yes, I know." Thomas smiled and reached for the wine. "Can I refresh your glass for you?"

Annabel only nodded, holding out her glass toward him, her gaze still on the food before her.

When the idea to create a meal made of her favorite foods first came to him, Thomas wasn't sure it was a good one, but seeing Annabel's reaction was just what he'd hoped for.

"But how?" She finally looked at him after setting her glass down. "How did you know?"

"After you left the hospital yesterday I stopped by ROOTS, introduced myself to your sister Abby, and asked what your favorite foods are." He decided the direct approach was best. "Then I made arrangements to have them served tonight for us."

Annabel's gaze dropped back to the table. The candlelight danced over her shocked features and when she captured her bottom lip with her teeth, Thomas wanted nothing more than to lean across the table and release the fullness from its imprisonment.

And cover her mouth with his.

"Does this mean we're having strawberry chocolate devil's food cake for dessert?" she asked, cutting into the steak.

Thomas laughed, loving the playfulness in her eyes. "You'll just have to wait and see."

The meal was terrific and they talked while they

ate, sharing stories that covered everything from childhood experiences to college escapades. When dessert arrived, Annabel claimed she was too stuffed to eat, but the cake was perfectly sized for two and they managed to make a pretty good dent in it.

"Mmm, that is just too delicious for words," Annabel purred after sliding her fork from between her lips. "This has got to be the best meal I've ever had."

"I'm in complete agreement with you." Thomas signaled for the server, who came into the room. "Do you think we could meet the chef? We'd like to thank him for this amazing meal."

"I'll see if he's available."

A few minutes later a tall man with black hair arrived at their table. "I'm Shane Roarke, the executive chef here at the Gallatin Room."

Thomas introduced himself and Annabel, offering his compliments before his date took over the conversation as only Annabel could, with charm and grace.

"I can't believe Thunder Canyon was able to lure you away from the big city, Mr. Roarke," Annabel said after the man admitted to working in Los Angeles, San Francisco and Seattle before taking his current position at the resort.

Thomas noticed the quick tightening of the chef's jaw for a moment, but then the man blinked and it was gone. "Well, I've only been here since June, but I'm finding I like the slower pace of Thunder Canyon," Shane said. "I'm glad you enjoyed your meal."

The man left and Thomas saw Annabel's gaze follow him as he walked away. A flare of heat raced through him that could only be jealousy, but Thomas quickly squashed the emotion.

"I need to tell my cousin DJ about him," Annabel said, turning her attention back to the dessert. "I think they would get along great."

"Why's that?" Thomas asked.

"DJ owns the Rib Shack, another restaurant here in the resort. Not that he could get Mr. Roarke to work for him, but he'll probably try." She took another mouthful of cake and then laid the fork on the plate. "Oh, this really is so good, but I can't possibly eat another bite. I've probably gained five pounds from one meal."

"How about we work some of that off by dancing?"

Annabel's shocked gaze locked with his. "Dancing?"

The idea surprised Thomas just as much the moment the words left his mouth, but right now he wanted nothing more than to hold this woman in his arms.

"Why not? There's wonderful music coming from the main area and we've got plenty of room." Thomas stood and held out his hand.

"Oh, I'm not the best dancer." Annabel sat back in her chair, the candlelight highlighting the pretty blush on her cheeks. "The whole two left feet thing."

"Maybe you just haven't met the right partner yet." He waited, knowing it wouldn't take her long to match up his words with her earlier declaration about him not having met the right dog. "Dance with me, Annabel. Please."

She placed her hand in his and Thomas gently pulled her to her feet and into his arms. He easily maneuvered her until they were in front of the windows again, the star-filled night sky a beautiful backdrop to the dimly lit room.

Her left hand rested at his shoulder and he tucked her other hand in his and brought both of them to rest over his heart. The softness of her hair brushed against his jaw and he inhaled, pulling her sexy vanilla scent deep into his chest. His hand flattened across her back, seeming to startle her, but he just pressed her tighter to him, her curves wreaking havoc with his attempts at controlling his libido.

Despite all the time they'd spent together over the past two weeks, and the few times they touched, they'd never been this close.

Thomas now knew why he'd worked so hard to keep distance between them. Holding Annabel in his arms wasn't like anything he'd ever felt before.

And that scared the hell out of him.

"You are a liar, Miss Cates."

"Am I?" Her words caressed his neck with warm breaths.

"You're a wonderful dancer." Thomas lowered

his head a few inches until his cheek rested against hers. "I think you like keeping me off balance where you're concerned."

"Now why would I do that?"

He leaned back, hating how their bodies separated, but wanting to see her eyes. "I don't know. I'm normally not a man who likes surprises."

"Well then, what I'm about to say next shouldn't be a surprise," she said, looking up at him, "but I'm going to tell you anyway."

He stilled, having absolutely no idea what she was going to say.

"This has been the most magical night of my life, Thomas." Annabel gazed at him, her eyes wide. "Thank you…from the bottom of my heart."

Annabel had no idea what time it was when Thomas pulled his sleek sports car to a stop in her family's driveway.

The last time she'd looked at the glowing digits of the car's clock it had been almost eleven-thirty. That had been when they left the resort, and as hard as she tried, Annabel just couldn't keep her eyes open during the drive home.

They'd stayed at the restaurant for another hour after her heartfelt thank-you that she'd been so sure would end in a kiss.

Only she hadn't been brave enough to rise up on her tiptoes and press her mouth to his.

Instead Thomas had replied with a simple "you're welcome" and they continued to dance until coffee arrived, which they enjoyed while finishing off the last of that decadent cake.

He shut off the engine and the car stilled. She heard him turn toward her, but again, her eyelids were too heavy even though she'd love to see the expression on his face.

"Annabel?"

He spoke her name in a soft whisper that sent shivers up and down her spine. Something she'd been experiencing from the moment he walked onto her front porch dressed in a charcoal-gray suit that fit him to perfection. Heck, even her sisters had sighed as they peeked at him through the dining-room window.

"Are you asleep?" he asked, his voice back to its normal level, which was still sexy.

"No, but if I lived another mile or so away I probably would be." This time she succeeded in opening her eyes and smiled. "Did I thank you for an amazing evening?"

"Many times."

"Good." She closed her eyes and stretched, pointing her naked toes in a perfect arch. The heels had slipped off the moment she got into his car. The pair were her favorite, but she didn't wear them too often.

Or this dress, because while she loved what the

bandage-style dress did for her curves, it tended to ride up whenever she sat.

Or stretched.

The sound of the driver's side door opening and the inside light coming on had Annabel bolting upright in her seat. She grabbed the hem and yanked it back into place before looking at Thomas, but he was already out of the car.

The interior went dark again when he closed the door, but she'd found her purse, shawl and shoes by the time he walked around the car.

Sliding out of the passenger seat, she gently closed the door behind her. Except for the porch light at the kitchen door, the house was dark and the last thing she wanted was an audience when she and Thomas said good-night.

"I was going to get the door— Hey, you're shorter."

Annabel smiled and held up her shoes dangling from her fingers. "Sore tootsies."

"You okay to walk in bare feet?"

"Of course. I'm outside all the time— Thomas!" Annabel felt the ground disappear beneath her feet as Thomas lifted her into his arms and headed for the side porch.

"We can't—" he paused and cleared his throat, his grip tightening on her bare thighs "—can't take any chances."

She looped her arm around his shoulders, grateful when she didn't knock him in the head with her purse. Moments later, they stood in the soft glow of the light and he gently set her feet to the ground, his arm staying around her waist.

Her hand slid to his upper arm, but she tightened her hold, keeping their bodies close, hating that her other hand was filled with her shawl and shoes.

"There you go. Home safe and sound."

She tried to read the emotion in his gaze, but he dipped his head, the shadows making it impossible for her to see.

Did it matter?

Was he finally going to kiss her?

"Thanks for tonight," he finally said, releasing her and stepping away. "I haven't had… It was a great night."

The lump of disappointment in her throat when he made no move to give her a good-night kiss made it impossible for Annabel to speak. She could only nod as she reached for the screen door.

He stepped off the porch and she spun around, opening the inside door and slipping into the kitchen before he even made it back to the driveway.

Not knowing why she did, Annabel stood at the door and watched through the window as he climbed back into his car and started the engine.

What had gone wrong?

Tonight had been pure magic from the moment he'd picked her up. He'd been gracious with her family, attentive to the point of distraction from the first moment he touched her and that meal—who goes to the effort of making sure they had a private table, finding out a date's favorite foods...

He should've kissed her.

She should've kissed him.

She dumped her stuff on the counter beside her, her hand hovering over the light switch, and still his car stayed.

Was he waiting for her to—

She dragged her fingers downward, flipping the lever and the porch went dark. Then she twisted the lock on the door, the click echoing in the quiet.

Suddenly the car's engine cut off, and Thomas emerged, sprinting back across the drive. She undid the lock, yanked open the door and pushed at screen. Seconds later, he had her wrapped in his arms as he pushed her up against the wall, his mouth covering hers in a searing kiss.

Her hands plunged into his hair, pulling him closer and loving how his kiss was thorough, possessive and exploded with an intensity that had started the moment they met. His hands moved lower until they cupped her backside, pulling her tight to him. He leaned into her, lifted her until their bodies aligned perfectly, allowing her to feel the evidence of his arousal.

She moaned low in her throat, their tongues stroking against each other, eager to share the heat and hunger. He echoed that moan back to her with his own, and regret pulsated through her because she knew they had to stop.

Finally, he lifted his head, his hands sliding back to her waist. He pressed his forehead to hers, his rapid breathing matching her own as her hands moved to lie against the restless rise and fall of his chest.

"Wow." Annabel stole another kiss, thrilling at the groan the quick swipe of her lips over his brought forth. "Please, tell me we are going to do this again. And soon."

Thomas's laugh was husky and warm. "What's that? Go out for dinner?"

"Yeah, that, too." Especially if this man were on the menu as appetizer, main course and dessert because she was already craving another taste of heaven.

Chapter Eight

"I think you're doing what mothers do best, sticking your nose where it doesn't belong."

Annabel stilled as her father's voice carried from the kitchen to the stairway.

Wednesdays were her late days at the library so she'd taken a run without Smiley this morning—his habit of stopping at every tree made it a bit hard to maintain a good pace. When she'd returned she'd grabbed a mug of freshly brewed java and her mail from the basket in the hall before heading up the stairs to her bedroom.

Until her father's pronouncement stopped her in her tracks.

"Annabel doesn't have a lot of experience when it comes to men," came a more feminine voice—her mother. "I'm worried she's going to get hurt."

Unable to resist, Annabel sat on a step and waited, sure her sisters had shown up as well and, like the rest of the family, they'd have no problem stating their own opinions about her love life.

Or anything else, for that matter.

"Then why don't you talk to her?" Zeke Cates said. "No one else is home, including me, because I'm on my way out. You can say your piece without it becoming a major discussion."

Bless her dad. He understood how hard it was at times to be part of a big family. Annabel loved her parents and siblings, and living in the house where she grew up made financial sense, but there were times when having space to yourself and a sense of privacy were sorely lacking.

"But she'll think I'm interfering."

"You are, dear, but that's your right as her mother."

Annabel smiled at her father's parting words, knowing the following silence was her parents sharing a goodbye kiss.

Yep, there was the slam of the kitchen door.

Now, should she go back to the kitchen and find out exactly what was bothering her mother or scoot upstairs and see what Smiley was up to since he hadn't made an appearance yet? She still needed to grab a shower—

"Oh, there you are."

Busted.

Annabel took another sip of coffee, enjoying the surprise on her mother's face. "Here I am. Good morning."

"Good morning, dear." Her mother held on to her own coffee mug with a grip so tight Annabel feared the handle would crack. "How was your run?"

"It was good." Annabel eyed the clock hanging on the wall. She had plenty of time before she had to leave for work. Might as well get this over with. "So, tell me why you're so worried about me."

"Oh, Annabel...I'm sorry you overheard that." Her mother sighed. "I'm just concerned that you're falling too fast for your doctor friend."

Her doctor friend. Well, that was one way of looking at what was happening between her and Thomas. After the way he went out of his way to create such a special dinner—and the way he'd kissed her goodnight last Saturday—she'd like to think he was at least a step above being a friend.

A big step.

"Thomas and I are...getting to know one another. So I would hold off on ordering the wedding invitations just yet."

Her mother walked up the stairs and sat beside her. "You like him."

"Of course I like him. The man is smart, funny, caring and gorgeous. What's not to like?"

"I will admit he was very nice when we met him the other night, even if he did seem a bit serious. Have you seen him since your date?"

Annabel wondered where her mother was heading with that question. "Yes, of course I have."

"At the hospital."

"Yes, at the hospital. I stopped in on Monday to talk about the Tuesday and Thursday sessions I'll be having with Smiley, and I saw him again yesterday after the session."

"Are you planning to go over there today?"

As a matter of fact she was, during her dinner break. Annabel wanted to check on Mr. Owens, whose visit with Smiley yesterday was cut short because the elderly man hadn't been feeling well.

"Yes, I am, but to visit a friend, Mom. Not to see Thomas."

"Don't you think it's strange that outside of your two dates, you've only seen him at the hospital?"

"It's where he works. Not to mention where the therapy sessions take place. Doesn't it make sense that's where we would run into each other?"

"It seems to me you are the one doing all the running into, not him."

Okay, that hit home. Annabel took another sip from her mug, silently acknowledging her mother had a point.

She hadn't heard from Thomas at all on Sunday, even though he'd left with a whispered "I'll call you" after that mind-blowing, body-numbing kiss that really did make her wish she had her own place.

Stopping by his office on Monday to see Marge made sense as the secretary was coordinating Smiley's sessions. Of course, Thomas was there and he did seem happy to see her. They'd even gone down to the hospital café for a light dinner.

At her suggestion.

And he'd walked the two of them all the way to her car yesterday after she'd run into him when leaving Mr. Owens's room.

He'd teased her about parking in the farthest corner of the lot. She'd flirted back that maybe she'd been trying to lure him away from the crowds.

His smile had disappeared when he took a step closer, crowding her against her car. Annabel had been so sure he was going to kiss her again. Until Smiley had broken the spell by noticing a nearby squirrel and uncharacteristically taking off in pursuit.

Okay, so she'd only seen Thomas at the hospital the past few days, but that didn't stop the man from invading her dreams at night.

She wanted to kiss him again. She wanted more than that. The idea of stripping off that starched dress shirt and perfectly matched tie to find out just what those shoulders of his looked like—

"Annabel?"

Wow, she'd gotten lost there for a moment. "Sorry about that, Mom. Did you say something?"

"It's just that your social life has been a bit slow lately and you don't want to rush—"

"Slow?" Annabel cut off her mother's words with a sharp laugh. "Mom, I haven't dated anyone steady in over three years."

"Which is why I'm concerned that you're doing what you always do. You jump in with both feet when you believe in something, without much thought as to how difficult things might become in the future. Whether it's upgrading the children's area of the library or the therapy training with Smiley."

Yes, those projects had entailed a lot of hard work and effort on her part, coupled with more steps backward than forward at times thanks to the said "both feet" habit, but she'd accomplished both goals, quite successfully she might add. "Hey, both of those other ventures turned out fine. Better than fine."

"Well then, what about when you decided to enter the Frontier Days marathon after only running a few weeks? You ended up in the E.R. with a stress fracture. Or that spur-of-the-moment road trip you and Jazzy took last summer that found you in the middle of nowhere with a busted engine?"

Annabel let loose a deep sigh. Boy, what were mothers for if not to remind you of your shortcomings? "So let's add getting a little starry-eyed over a doctor to the list."

"I'm just worried you're setting yourself up for heartache," her mother persisted, laying a hand on her arm. "Doctors are notorious for not having happy, stable marriages. I want you to be happy, just like I want all my children to be."

Surprised at her mother's claim, Annabel could only stare at her. "That's absurd. Where did you hear that about doctors' marriages?"

"I was chatting with Mrs. Banning the other day—"

"You talked about me with the neighbors?"

"Of course not. We were just visiting and she mentioned her daughter's marriage was ending, and in a very messy way. Her husband is a surgeon. He works terrible hours and wasn't there for her or the children. Now he's decided that the woman who supported him all through medical school is too boring to spend the rest of his life with."

"I'm sorry for what Mrs. Banning's daughter is going through, but it sounds as though there are more issues with that marriage than her husband's working hours."

"Mrs. Callahan was with us, too, and she mentioned a friend whose daughter also married a doctor right here in Thunder Canyon, who was crushed when her husband recently announced he was leaving her so he could marry one of the nurses on his staff. A much younger nurse."

"Who needs reality television when the Thunder Canyon gossip mill is alive and well?" Annabel rolled her eyes. "What about Cade and Abby? Cade has his own business and he works all kind of crazy hours."

"Cade works for his family, he can set his own hours. Besides, your sister was in love with Cade for years before she, or he, ever admitted their feelings."

"And Laila?" Annabel pushed harder, bringing up her other recently married sister. "Jackson is an executive at Traub Oil Industries and from what I've heard he travels a lot. Are you telling me Laila should be worried because they only knew each other a month before getting engaged?"

"By the time your sister met Jackson she'd had more experience when it came to men than all of my girls combined, although Jazzy is giving her a good run for her money. When Jackson came to town and swept Laila off her feet, they were both ready for married life."

Annabel stood. She was *ready* for this conversation to be over. Yes, everything her mother said about her sisters was true, but that didn't mean she was heading for heartache.

"Well, you don't have to worry because Thomas and I are...I don't know what we are, but we aren't thinking about anything close to marriage. I appreciate your concern, Mom, but I'm an adult and it's my life and my decision."

"Oh, honey, I just want you to be careful with your heart."

Evelyn Cates pushed to her feet as well, and Annabel saw nothing but love and concern in her mother's gaze.

"I am being careful," she said, leaning over to give her mom a quick kiss on the cheek. "Trust me, I'm not in over my head. And neither is my heart."

Thomas was so far over his head he didn't have a clue what he was going to do.

About Annabel.

Intentionally skipping the "Smiley Session" this afternoon had been the right decision. He was a busy man with a lot of work to do, which was why he was still sitting at his desk an hour after his official workday was over. An hour after Annabel and Smiley had left the hospital, thanks to Marge's report, who was working late herself.

Because of him.

The woman never left the office until he did. He'd told her often enough that it wasn't necessary for her to stay so late. But with her husband gone and her kids moved away, Marge always said the only things waiting for her at home were three cats and they'd survive just fine without her.

Him? She wasn't so sure of.

So most nights he went home with a briefcase full

of work or he'd circle back after grabbing a quick dinner off the hospital campus.

He sighed, leaned back in his chair and scrubbed at his tired eyes. He should get the heck out of here. Reading the same paragraph over and over again in his patient's file wasn't helping the information stick in his head.

Maybe because that space was already filled with images of a perky, bubbly blonde who'd taken his breath away the moment he'd pulled her into his arms and finally kissed her.

He'd thought about little else after they'd danced at the Gallatin Room. No, that wasn't true. He'd been thinking about kissing Annabel from the moment he'd met her, but last Saturday, the need and want had been building all night. Until he couldn't take it anymore.

There'd been so many chances.

Like when they'd walked to his car after leaving the resort or when he'd pulled into her family's driveway and discovered she wasn't asleep like he'd thought. Not to mention, when he'd set her back on her feet beneath the porch light after he'd carried her to the front door, her body brushing the length of his.

He'd taken none of those openings, having decided during the few minutes it took to reach her front porch it was best to keep things simple. Say good-night and leave. He managed to do both, but only made it as far as turning on the engine, before the porch light went out after Annabel got inside.

He'd missed his chance.

Seconds later, he'd been racing across the yard. The way the door opened immediately said she'd been watching him—waiting. It fanned the flames of his desire for her even higher.

The sureness of how it felt to hold her had taken its time to settle in, thanks to the passion of that kiss, but when it had, Thomas knew he had to get out of there. So he'd given a simple promise to call and then left.

Only he'd never called.

He'd seen Annabel on Monday here at the hospital and they'd grabbed a quick bite together down in the café—not the most private venue—and of course he heard about it the next day from a few colleagues. And while he'd purposely dropped by Mr. Owens's room on Tuesday to see how the visit went with Smiley, he hadn't planned on walking her and her dog out to the parking lot.

It'd just been so easy to talk to her. Thomas rose from behind his desk and walked to the window, drawn to the vivid reds and oranges of the setting sun.

No matter what the subject, Annabel made him feel relaxed and comfortable. Not to mention the crackle of sexual energy that seemed to surround her, a deep pulsing pull that called to him every time he saw her.

But late Tuesday night, after he found himself lying alone in his bed, wishing she was with him and, in turn, had berated himself for feeling that way again, he'd realized the simple truth.

Being with Annabel scared him silly.

Not that he was *with* her.

Two dinners and spending time together at the hospital didn't exactly make them a couple. Of course, Marge or some of the staff didn't need much more than to see them together in the hospital café to come to that conclusion.

Getting involved in a relationship again was the last thing he wanted, or needed, at the moment. He still felt he had to prove himself, to right the wrongs of his past, but he was having a hell of time keeping Annabel out of his head.

"So, what'll it be tonight?"

Marge's voice from the open doorway cut into his thoughts. He turned and found her flipping through the notebook she kept of take-out menus from the local restaurants.

"Chinese or Mexican?" she continued, not looking up at him. "Or are you not planning to stick around much longer?"

He didn't get a chance to choose.

"Mmm, go with the Chinese. The kung pao chicken at Mr. Lee's is to die for."

The lilting voice from his dreams drew his attention past his secretary. "Annabel. What are you doing here?"

Silence filled the air for a moment until Marge cleared her throat. "I think I'll just go down to the lounge and get myself a cup of hot tea. Annabel, would you like anything?"

"No, thanks, Marge, but I appreciate the offer."

Marge smiled at Annabel, shot him a quick wink over her shoulder that caused his stomach to drop to his feet and left the office area.

Oh, hell, maybe it was the sight of Annabel walking toward him in a simple cotton skirt, tank top and wedged heels that did that.

Or the fire-engine red polish on her toes.

He bit back a groan and forced his gaze back above her neckline. "So, what brings you this way so late?"

Annabel waved what looked like the remains of a tattered teddy bear in the air. "I had to come back for Smiley's baby."

Her words threw him. "Excuse me?"

"I know it doesn't look like much now, but this stuffed bear came with Smiley from the shelter." As she glanced down at the toy, her long golden curls tumbled over one shoulder. "He carried it around for weeks after I first brought him home. Then he seemed to only need the thing when he went to sleep."

She offered a quick shrug, and continued, "I don't know why he brought it with him to today's session, but once we got home I realized he'd left it behind. I had to run a few errands anyway. When I pulled into the parking lot, I saw your light was on, so I thought I'd stop by and see if you wanted to grab some dinner…"

Her voice trailed off when she looked at him again. Thomas swallowed hard at the mixture of desire and awareness he read in her blue eyes as their gazes locked. And just like that his world tilted off balance as uncontrolled need and want washed over him again.

Shoving his hands deep in his pockets, Thomas broke free and looked away. "Annabel, I'm not sure that is such a good idea."

"What's not a good idea? Chinese? Hey, if you want Mexican, that's fine with me. I'm easy."

Damn it, the last thing she was doing was making this easy.

Control.

He needed to get this situation back under control, back to what he was used to, a place of organization—of having power over one's actions and emotions.

A place that was familiar to him, ever since his mother pulled him aside after his grandfather's accident and told him tears were not allowed. At the tender age of seven, she'd expected him to handle what happened to his grandfather with the same dignity and grace that the Norths handled everything else.

Which probably explained why he'd thrown himself into his studies, determined that when he became a doctor, no one else would suffer the way his grandfather had. Of course, he'd learned the hard way that doctors weren't miracle workers, but he had a pretty damn good track record so far, at least here at TC General.

If his affair with Victoria had taught him anything, it was that he had the tendency of letting a woman's beauty blind him to everything else around. Considering his lack of judgment and having to learn to live with the regret, the last thing he wanted was to make the same mistake.

He faced her again. "I've got a lot of work ahead of me and now that your dog therapy sessions are in place, I don't think— It's just that my free time is going to be very limited."

Barely a heartbeat passed before Annabel offered him a bright smile. "Oh. Well, you've obviously given this a lot of thought." Her cheery tone and calm acceptance were the last things he expected. "I don't want to make things...difficult for you. I'll just go and let you get back to work."

Thomas wanted to speak, even though he had no idea what else to say. Not that it mattered. His throat was so constricted he could barely breathe.

A nod was all he managed.

She quickly backed up until she reached the door. "So, I guess I'll see you when I see you."

Then she was gone.

Thomas stood rooted to the spot, his blood pounding in his temples at he stared at the empty space. Had he really just told a beautiful and fascinating woman he wasn't interested?

He waited for the cool detachment that told him he'd done the right thing to bring relief that it was over. It was nowhere to be found. In its place instead was an overwhelming rush of regret and panic that filled every ounce of his being.

"Dr. North?"

The sharp tone in Marge's voice caused his head to snap up.

How long had she been standing there? How long had he been standing here staring at the doorway like a fool?

He started to ask, but had to pause and clear his throat first. "Ah, I don't know how much of that you overheard, but for some reason I think I should—"

"Go."

With one word the despair shifted to hope. "She has no reason to let me—"

"What she has is a good head start." Marge folded her hands primly over her stomach. "And you're without a car today, if memory serves. Go."

Thomas automatically reached across his desk for his phone and house keys. "I need to shut down—"

"Turning off a computer, the lights and locking your door is within my scope of abilities." She made a show of glancing at her watch. "If you're not back in fifteen minutes, I'm going home."

Sprinting past his secretary, Thomas headed for the stairs. He raced outside and into the parking lot, praying Annabel was a creature of habit and had parked in the same location as before.

He hoped he hadn't ruined his chance with her. If he had, he'd have a lot of making up to do.

Chapter Nine

Annabel couldn't believe how much Thomas's words hurt.

She'd thought things were going so well between them. They hadn't run into each other when she popped in to check on Mr. Owens yesterday, and while she'd hoped to see him today at Smiley's session, it never occurred to her that he'd been avoiding her.

Obviously it hadn't come to mind or she'd have never made the effort to seek him out tonight.

Coming back for Smiley's toy hadn't been an urgent issue. The dog hadn't even noticed it was gone, but Annabel foolishly took it as a sign.

So she'd changed her clothes, spritzed her wrists and cleavage with her favorite perfume and hopped back in her car, daydreaming about more alone time with Thomas and hoping she'd have the good fortune of finding him still at the hospital.

Oh, she'd found him all right.

Shoving the ratty teddy bear in her bag, Annabel marched across the parking lot, proud that she'd at least stayed cool during his little speech and walked away with her head held high.

Okay, so she walked fast once she left his office, but still she managed to keep it together in the elevator, thankful she hadn't run into anyone. She still didn't understand what drove him to say what he did, but the bottom line was the coming days would be empty without him.

The tears began to well in her eyes.

"Hey, wait!"

A voice calling from behind her, followed by hands closing over her shoulders, sent a rush of panic through her. A quick, sharp jab with her elbow was on the mark, punctuated by a male grunt and she was free. Spinning around, keys laced between her fingers, Annabel took a defensive stance ready to scream—

"Thomas!" She dropped her hands, but not before quickly swiping the remaining moisture from her eyes. "Are you crazy? I could have stabbed you with my keys!"

"I'm sorry…didn't mean to scare you." He puffed out the words while rubbing his hand across his midsection. "That was a stupid…stupid thing to do."

At least the man was right about something tonight.

Annabel folded her arms under her breasts, tried to slow her runaway breathing while telling herself he deserved the hard poke to the gut. "Yes, it was."

"No, I don't mean grabbing you— Well, yes, that was dumb, too." He dropped his hand, but then propped both on his hips. "I'm talking about what happened in my office. I don't know what I was saying. I mean, I know what I said. I heard the words coming out of my mouth. It's just that I've been doing a lot of thinking the past couple of weeks, hell, the past couple of years. Probably too much thinking, but I've been that way since I was a kid."

Annabel blinked hard and tried to keep up with Thomas's ramblings. He didn't mean to scare her, but he did follow her out here. Pretty quickly, too, as she'd only walked out of his office less than ten minutes ago.

She ignored the sharp thrill that zinged through her.

"The thing is, I think I was too hasty. It's just that I've been trying to work through some things from the past and what's been going on between us. You know, weighing the good, the bad, lessons learned, and all that stuff. The next thing I knew you were standing there—"

"Thomas, stop!"

Annabel took a leap of faith that she finally understood what this man was trying to say.

He did as she asked, but the silence only made his words a bigger jumbled mess in her head. She didn't want to sort through them right now. Not with him standing right there in front of her.

Grabbing his already loosened tie, and throwing her concerns—and her mother's admonitions—to the wind, she wrapped it once around her palm and yanked him up against her. "Are you going to kiss me or what?"

He blinked owlishly, then relief filled his eyes, his hooded gaze dropping to her lips. "God, yes."

She didn't wait, but instead rose to her toes and covered his mouth with hers before pulling back just enough to gently suck his lower lip between hers.

His large, capable hands circled her waist, holding her in place as a deep groan rumbled in his chest. He quickly took over, ravishing her mouth with hot, deep skims of his tongue against hers. She boldly matched his every move, surrendering to the craziness of the moment.

And it was crazy.

He pressed her up against her car door, his hips brushing in a slow back and forth motion that brought forth a husky moan of her own. A delicious ache for more, much more, filled her, spreading like wildfire until every corner of her body vibrated with need.

His mouth slipped from hers, his lips trailing across her cheek to her ear. "I know how insane this sounds, but I want you, Annabel."

A victorious thrill raced through her and she couldn't hold back the nervous giggle that escaped. "Well, I would say your place or mine, but I'm afraid my father would be blocking your path, his shotgun firmly in hand."

Thomas leaned back, an unreadable emotion in his eyes. Then he blinked and it was replaced with an amused gleam. "Then I guess we'd better go to my place. Problem is my car is in the shop."

Annabel jiggled her keys in front of him. "You know, I'm not even going to ask how you planned to get home tonight. You want to drive or play navigator?"

He gave her a crooked grin as he slipped the keys from her hand. "We can decide that later, but for now, it'll be faster if I drive."

Less than fifteen minutes later they pulled into his condo's garage, located in an upscale complex Annabel had never been to before. When he went to shut off the engine, she slipped her fingers from his, smiling at how they'd became entangled in the first place. Seemed a little teasing finger action back and forth across his powerful thigh was too much of a distraction for the sexy doctor.

But she couldn't help herself.

The man drove her quirky little bug as if it was a luxury car, with purpose and speed. What could she say? It was a turn-on.

"Nice place," she said, popping out of the passenger side as the garage door slid silently closed behind them.

"It's just the garage," Thomas shot back, taking her hand again as he headed for the stairs. "Wait until you see the master bedroom."

At the top of the stairs, he opened a door and wrapping his arm around her waist, pulled her close and kissed her again. She clung to him as he walked her backward into what she guessed was the front foyer.

He broke free of their kiss and flipped on the lights. She blinked as everything came into focus. Then she gazed around in curiosity.

Soft lighting highlighted fine leather furniture and the shiny chrome and glass tables that sat atop an oversize plush Oriental rug her toes itched to dig into. The best "boy toys" money could buy filled the room, as well. An enormous flat-screen TV hung over an empty fireplace while nearby floor-to-ceiling bookshelves held numerous black boxes that must be a high-end stereo system.

Gleaming hardwood floors stretched the length of the room, including a dining area with a table big enough to seat six. Off to the left, she saw a kitchen.

His home was beautiful, but her first thought was "professional decorator." She wondered how much of Thomas was even reflected here.

"Please don't tell me you want a tour." He nuzzled her from behind, his lips warm against her neck, and Annabel was glad she'd secured her hair to one side with a large clip. "If so, let's start with the second floor."

She couldn't agree more, with one minor change.

Facing him again, she dropped her purse to the floor and quickly stripped off his tie, tossing it to one side. "Oh, I think we'll start—and finish—right here."

It seemed to take a moment for Thomas to get her meaning, but once he did, he lifted her in his arms and headed straight for the sofa.

Anticipation flooded her insides as she kicked off her shoes along the way, waiting until he sat, her straddling his lap before she leaned in and captured his mouth again.

Just like she'd hoped to do in his office.

While their mouths tasted and nipped, devoured and shared, her fingers went to work on the buttons of his dress shirt, releasing them all the way to his waist. Yanking the material open as far as it would go, she reveled in the feel and heat of his naked chest, at the way he jumped at her touch.

Time to get serious.

When she lightly dragged her fingernails over

his nipples, his hands gripped her hips, cradling her heated center over the thick ridge of his arousal. The loose swing of her skirt made sure that the only barrier between her nakedness and the silkiness of his slacks were the simple thong panties she wore. Unable to resist, she rotated her hips in a slow circle.

"Damn, that feels good," he rasped, breaking free of their kiss. "You feel good."

Their eyes met and held as he gently pulled her tank top free from the skirt's waistband, his hands slowly sliding underneath and up over her belly. He kept going, taking the material with him until she had no choice but to raise her arms as he tugged the top over her head.

While her hands were raised, she'd reached back and freed her hair, loving the heat in his eyes as her breasts pressed against the bra's lacy cups. Shaking her head sent loose waves flying over her shoulders, but it was the way his fingertips traced the delicate straps of her bra that sent shivers dancing over her skin.

"You cold?" His words came out in rough whisper. "The air-conditioning is pretty strong."

"I think it's more about what you're doing to me than artificial cooling." He proved her point when he caught the lobe of her ear gently between his teeth and another shudder rolled through her. "Oh, see what I mean?"

"Here, let's get you warm." In one swift move, he

had her flat on her back against the cool, soft leather of his sofa as he stretched out over her.

Soft except for the object pressing into her lower back.

"What the—" Annabel reached beneath her and pulled out a large rectangular object covered in buttons of all shapes, sizes and colors.

He took the device from her and tossed it to the side. "It's just my remote."

She gave a half laugh, lowering her voice to a purr. "A remote for what?"

Thomas deftly pulled down the zipper of her skirt while his lips left behind a trail of wet kisses over her collar bone. He then returned his focus to the lace edging of her bra, his tongue dipping inside the delicate border to wet the skin beneath. "Everything."

As sinfully wonderful as his focus was, Annabel persisted. "Everything?"

He groaned and lifted his head, bracing himself on one elbow. "Don't tell me you really want to know?"

Annabel shifted, his erection now in perfect alignment between her thighs. "Mmm, impress me."

"I thought I was."

She laughed, and he joined her, his deep chuckle vibrating the length of her body and at that moment, as sure as if her heart had flipped over and displayed the words *I Belong to Thomas North* etched in a pretty scrolled font, she knew.

She was in love with this crazy, wonderful man.

It wasn't a sentiment she had a lot of experience with, but the pure joy and elation pouring from her heart was something she planned to embrace with both hands and never let go of.

He surprised her when he reached over, picked the remote up and placed it back in her hand. "Press the numbers 3-1-7-3 on the bottom keypad."

Annabel did as instructed, focusing on the device. The last thing she wanted was Thomas to see the newfound emotion going off like skyrockets inside her before she had a chance to examine the feeling.

In private.

As soon as she pressed the last number, a fire blazed to life in the fireplace, blanketing the room with dancing shards of light and a warm glow.

"Oh!"

His lips nibbled up the side of her neck. "Now enter 6-8-7-4-2."

Her fingers shook as she pushed the correct buttons and seconds later a faint beep filled the air, before it was replaced with the smooth strains of classic jazz flowing from the stereo.

"Okay, I'm officially impressed." Annabel blinked hard, refusing to allow her head, or her heart, to even imagine Thomas showing these tricks to someone else. Mentally shaking off that thought, she playfully pointed the remote at him. "Now, what's the magic combination that works on you?"

A smile tipped one corner of his sensual mouth as he took the device from her hand and tossed it farther away this time in the direction of the closest chair. "I think you already know what buttons to press."

He pushed up to his knees and peeled off his shirt. Annabel found herself thankful for the fire's glow that showed off his wide shoulders and washboard abs to perfection. Next was his belt and darn if he didn't take his time letting the strip of leather slide from his belt loops.

Loosening the button at his waist, he reached for the zipper, but she brushed his hand away and slowly lowered the zipper.

She only caught a glimpse of dark boxer briefs and the length of him pressing against the material before he reached for her, tugging gently at her skirt. Raising her hips, he eased the material down over her legs, leaving her in nothing but her bra and matching panties.

"You are perfection, Annabel."

The naked desire in his gaze called to her. She crooked her finger in a come-hither motion and he quickly complied, molding his hard planes with her curves.

He took her mouth again as his fingers nimbly opened the front clash of her bra, his warm hand cupping her breast. His thumb rasped over the hardened bud, drawing it even tighter until he ended the kiss and drew the peak into the moist heat of his mouth.

A blast of shameless need flared deep inside her. Annabel arched, offering him more, and he took, moving his mouth from one breast to the other, leaving behind a shimmering wetness that tingled in the cool night air.

She reached low, her fingers brushing across his stomach as the need to touch him overpowered her. He shuddered when she slipped beneath the cotton waistband and curled around him. She stroked him once, twice, before he pulled her hand away.

"Don't," he rasped. "It's been…a while since I've done this."

His words made her heart soar. He released her wrist and she clutched at his shoulders as his fingers easily moved aside the damp material covering the most imitate part of her before slipping into her wet heat.

"Oh, for me, too. Thomas, please…"

Moments later, the rest of their clothes disappeared and Thomas paused only to sheathe himself with a condom he grabbed from his wallet. Then he was back between her legs, cupping her bottom and tilting her hips. He entered her with a long, slow thrust, capturing her gasp with his mouth.

Their bodies moved together in a natural, instinctive rhythm. A burning caught fire deep inside her, growing stronger and stronger, taking her higher with each demanding stroke.

Those same fireworks she'd felt deep inside from

the moment they met threatened to explode, shattering her heart and soul in a million colorful pieces.

His lips moved to her neck, whispering words against her skin, pushing her even higher as she dragged her nails over his back, demanding the sweet release only he could give.

Then the fuse of her passion ignited, sending her spiraling into the heavens. She clung to him, crying out his name, loving the moment when he gave up his last remnant of control, buried himself deep inside her, joining her.

They lay there together afterward, trying to catch their breaths and failing when he pressed his lips to the pulsing in her neck and she tightened around him.

Annabel had never known a moment like this before in her life. Was it because her heart had already laid claim to this charming, honest and dedicated man?

Her wonder was interrupted by their stomachs suddenly rumbling in sync. She laughed aloud, the sweetness of the moment almost too much to bear. "Boy, I guess you do want dinner."

"I'm starved." Thomas lifted himself off her while flashing a grin of total male satisfaction as he helped her sit up. "Even more so now."

"Chinese from Mr. Lee's still sounds good to me."

"Me, too." Thomas reached for his pants, pulled out his cell phone and hit the speed dial number. "Any special requests?"

"I'm happy with anything."

He rattled off a list of appetizers, his arched brows silently asking for her approval with each item. Annabel nodded in agreement as she scooped up her clothes, suddenly wishing for a light blanket to throw over her naked body.

Not that she was ashamed of being like this with him, but Thomas had been right. The air-conditioning was going at full blast and the air was chilly despite the fire.

Or was it reality setting in?

Goodness knows, she had no idea where things were headed between them now, other than dinner and hopefully more moments like what they just shared.

But what did this mean to Thomas?

She still wasn't sure exactly what he'd been trying to tell her back in his office, or the parking lot. Did he want more? Did he want her? Could he possibly love her in return?

"Okay, we're all set."

Thomas's words pulled her from her thoughts. He stood, the cool air obviously not affecting him, and then before she realized what he was doing, he easily lifted her into his arms.

"Hey!"

"You think I'm going to let some high school delivery boy get an eyeful by staying downstairs? No way." He gave her a quick squeeze. "Besides, we've got twenty minutes until the food gets here."

Annabel laughed again. "You've got to stop carrying me around."

"You feel…good in my arms."

She cupped his face with both hands and placed a chaste kiss, one that carried all the love in her heart, on his mouth. He carried her up the stairs to his bedroom and laid her on the silky comforter. Never breaking eye contact, Thomas lowered his mouth to hers, returning her kiss with one that was just as soft and sweet, even more so because of the slight tremble when his lips met hers.

Sunlight tried to make its way through the room-darkening shades with little success. Exactly how Thomas preferred it on those few mornings when he tried to sleep in.

Like today. Lying on his stomach, he cracked open one eye to focus on his bedside clock: 8:00 a.m.

Blinking hard, he looked again. That had to be wrong. For him, sleeping in usually meant staying in bed until six, six-thirty at the latest.

Nope, the numbers were an eight, a zero and now a one.

He bolted upright, coming to a fast realization of two things. The first, he was alone in his king-size bed, even though that's not the way he'd gone to sleep last night. The second was the aroma of frying bacon hovering in the air.

Annabel.

He quickly grabbed his cell phone from the bed-side table, and checked his calendar. He breathed a sigh of relief. Yes, his first appointment of the day wasn't scheduled until noon.

Pulling on a pair of briefs and sweats, he stopped to use the bathroom and brush his teeth. After toss-ing his toothbrush back into the holder, he paused and stared into the mirror, his reflected image blur-ring as he thought back to the madness and passion that had consumed him last night.

They hadn't even made it past his living-room sofa that first time. Not that he was complaining. Being with Annabel had been amazing, and after-ward, they'd spent the rest of the night in his bed, sharing Chinese takeout, a bottle of wine and each other.

Not the evening he'd thought he'd have after the way he'd fumbled through explaining his "I'm too busy" speech. A decision that hadn't lasted all of five minutes before he chased after her. Did she un-derstand any of what he'd tried to say? Both in his office and in the parking lot?

Hell, he wasn't sure *he* understood the logic and reasoning that still swirled inside his head when it came to her, them.

But she'd dismissed his ramblings with a hard

kiss, and he'd thrown caution, and control, out the window.

Yet again. Letting down his guard like that was something he hadn't done since—

Refusing to confuse things even more with thoughts of the past, Thomas stalked out of the bathroom and followed his nose downstairs. He started across the living room when he noticed a blanket draped over one of the chairs—a patchwork quilt, done up in rectangular-shaped blocks in shades of brown, dark red, black and beige that reminded him of the glass-tile pattern in his kitchen. Tucked into the folds of material was a dog-eared copy of a romance novel featuring a half-naked cowboy on the cover.

"Good morning, sleepyhead." Annabel strolled in from the kitchen, looking impossibly sexy wearing only his wrinkled dress shirt from last night and her long hair pulled back in a messy ponytail. "You saved me a trip back upstairs to get you. Hope you're hungry."

She set two plates piled with scrambled eggs, bacon and buttered toast on his dining-room table, drawing his eye to the vase brimming with daisies perched in the middle.

Daisies?

He hadn't realized he had that much food in his kitchen, but he was quite certain the flowers hadn't been there at all.

"Ah, yeah, I'm starved." Thomas ignored the quick twist in his gut and held up the quilt. "Where'd this come from?"

"I made it." Her voice carried over her shoulder as she disappeared back into the kitchen, and then returned with glasses of orange juice and silverware. "Pretty, isn't it?"

"Yes, but what's it doing here?"

"I couldn't figure out how to lower your air-conditioning when I got up this morning." She sat at the table and motioned for him to join her. "So I grabbed it from my car to wrap around myself. Come on, let's eat before all of this gets cold."

"The food and the flowers came out of your car, as well?"

A piece of bacon stilled halfway to her mouth. "Is that a problem?"

"No, just curious." Proud of his causal tone, Thomas sat opposite her.

"When I went to get the quilt I remembered I stopped at the store last night before coming to the hospital. The flowers needed water and I thought the groceries could camp out in your fridge until I left." She took a bite. "Then I saw the inside of your fridge and figured a healthy breakfast was needed. You do know those things are made to hold food, right?"

He smiled and the knot in his stomach eased.

Everything Annabel said made perfect sense. It

just threw him at how easily those things seemed at home here.

How easily she fit into his home.

And how much he liked it.

Chapter Ten

Three days later, Thomas stepped out of his car, having parked at the far end of the already-crowded driveway at the Cates family ranch.

Tightening his grip on the bottle of wine and the bouquet of flowers he'd brought, he silently counted the number of cars and pickup trucks scattered around.

Six in total, which meant at least two more would be coming. Sunday dinner with Annabel's family.

Her entire family.

Fighting the urge to turn and bolt, he forced himself to keep walking forward, remembering how Annabel had offered the invite just last night.

They'd been lying together on his couch watching their second choice in a classic black-and-white movie night. The screwball romantic comedy featuring Lucille Ball had been Annabel's choice after viewing one of his favorite Jimmy Stewart dramas.

Her words had been casual, not even glancing away from the movie as she spoke, but Thomas could tell by the way her arm had tightened over his stomach how much she wanted him to say yes.

And the sparkle in her eyes when he had accepted.

A thank-you kiss followed, and they never saw the closing credits of the movie. She'd finally left in the wee hours of the morning.

They spent the past three evenings together at his place, but thanks to Smiley, who was like a child to Annabel, she hadn't slept over again since that first night. Not that her family minded taking care of the dog, she assured him. She'd shared the text message she'd sent on Thursday to her sister Jazzy, asking her to make sure Smiley was fed and let outside in the morning, but Smiley was her dog, her responsibility.

Knowing she couldn't stay hadn't cooled their lovemaking; if anything the time they spent in his bed had been hotter and sexier because they didn't have all night to be together.

Still, Thomas found himself tempted to tell Annabel to bring Smiley with her the next time she came over if it meant he could hold her in his arms all night.

And didn't that rock the already wobbly ground beneath his feet?

Walking up to the same kitchen door where he'd kissed her like crazy a week ago, Thomas remembered Annabel's light quip the first night they'd made love about how her father would've been waiting with a shotgun. He hadn't been quite sure if she'd been joking or serious, but now he pushed those thoughts from his head. Thinking about sex and Annabel at this moment probably wasn't a good idea.

Looking down at the wine and flowers in his hands, he wondered again if they were a good idea. Raised by parents who always insisted a gift for the hostess was a requirement, he'd felt strange leaving his house empty-handed.

So he'd turned around and gone back, grabbed a bottle from his private collection and stopped along the way to pick up the flowers, just in case her parents didn't drink wine.

A deep breath, pulled in through his nose and slowly released, helped a little, but not as much as he'd hoped.

Damn, he shouldn't be this nervous.

Having already met half of her family, how bad could it be to spend an afternoon with all of them?

"Psst! Hey, doc. Over here."

Thomas turned and saw Annabel standing at the far end of the porch. She sent him a saucy grin and signaled for him to join her. He did and she took his face in her hands and pulled him close, their lips meeting in a long, slow kiss that Annabel tried to deepen, but he held back.

"Spoilsport," she teased.

"With the size of your family? And your father's shotgun? I think not."

She laughed. "You just keep on impressing me, Dr. North."

Thomas again refused to let his mind wander back to how he'd impressed her on the couch, in his bed and beneath the dual-headed shower over the weekend.

She stepped back and he admired the simple sundress she wore, bright colors splashed in a wavy, tie-dyed pattern that seemed perfect for the hot August afternoon. He was already sweating beneath his collared shirt, despite the short sleeves, but he doubted that had anything to do with the temperature.

"You know, when I invited you here today I forgot to ask you one thing."

The seriousness of her tone got his attention. "What's that?"

"Who's your favorite baseball team?"

That's what she needed to know? "Ah, the Dodgers, I guess."

"Hmm, Dad and Brody are Rockies fans. Well, it should be okay. We're still a few weeks out from the start of football."

"The preseason is already under way."

She waved off his words. "Preseason games don't count. Not around here."

Thomas didn't realize she was such a fan of professional sports. "Tell that to the guys on the field."

"Who's your favorite team?"

He guessed they were still talking about football. "The Broncos, of course."

Annabel graced him with a bright smile and grabbed his arm. "Perfect! Let's go join the others."

Instead of going inside the house, Annabel led him around the backyard and to a large stone patio. Numerous chairs sat scattered around a raised fire pit, piled with fresh cut wood. Two steps led up to the main area where tables, one covered in an array of dishes, and more chairs filled the space.

Another gut check and a deep reach for confidence. How could one family have so many members?

"Dr. North." Zeke Cates, Annabel's father, rose from one of the chairs and greeted them first. "Glad you could make it. It's good to see you again."

Thomas quickly maneuvered the flowers and wine into one hand so he could take the older man's outstretched one. "It's good to see you, too. Thank you for including me, Mr. Cates. And please call me Thomas."

The man's sharp gaze moved between Thomas and Annabel. He tightened his grip and held it for a long moment before releasing him. "You know anything about barbecuing, Thomas?"

Not sure if he remembered Zeke's greeting being quite so strong the first time they met, Thomas resisted the urge to flex his fingers. "Ah, no, sir. Not much."

"That's too bad. Dad can use all the help he can get." A younger version of Annabel's father walked past, a plate piled high with uncooked steaks, burgers and hot dogs in his hands. "Hey, we can use his surgical precision when it comes to slicing the meat."

"That's Brody, one of my many annoying siblings," Annabel said with a grin.

Thomas nodded and acknowledged the younger man he guessed to be in his early twenties with a wave. The flowers started to slip from his grip but then he realized Annabel had reached for them. He released his hold on the bouquet, but held tight to the bottle of wine.

"Oh, aren't these pretty!" She buried her nose in the fragrant stems. "Yellow roses, white mums and my favorites, daisies."

A whisper of unease tagged Thomas as he glanced at the flowers. He hadn't noticed the specific types in the cluster when he grabbed them at the local florist in town.

Daisies again?

"So, you've already figured out my daughter's favorite flowers? How sweet." Evelyn Cates joined them and, thanks to his training, Thomas immediately picked up on the hint of anxiety in her tone. The older woman placed a hand on her daughter's arm. "Annabel, let's go find a vase for those."

"Actually, the flowers are for you, ma'am." Thomas slipped the tissue-wrapped bunch from Annabel's grip and presented them, along with the wine, to her mother. "And this is from a winery that's been in my family, on my mother's side, for years. I hope you enjoy it."

"Thank you." The strain around the woman's mouth eased for a moment, but when she looked at Annabel, the lines deepened and her smile appeared forced. "This was very kind of you."

Still confused, Thomas looked at Annabel hoping she wasn't upset over the flowers, but she offered him a full-blown smile that he felt all the way to his toes as she leaned into him, giving his arm a squeeze.

"Annabel?" Her mother headed toward the double glass doors. "You coming?"

"Don't worry, we won't scare off the good doctor while you're gone." Jazzy, one of the two sisters Thomas had already met, stepped outside through the same doors. "Annabel, I'm letting Smiley out. He started freaking out as soon as he spotted— Oops, watch out!"

The warning came too late as seconds later Thomas let out a rush of air when two large paws landed right on his stomach.

"Smiley!" Annabel cried out and reached for the dog's collar. "Get down!"

"It's all right." Brushing her hand away, Thomas gently lifted the dog's paws, forcing the animal to rest back on his haunches. "Sit," he added, trying for a stern tone, just in case a verbal command was needed.

The dog obeyed, but stayed in the middle of all of them, tail wagging wildly, his attention solely on Thomas, with a few side glances at his owner.

Returning the dog's grin, Thomas reached down and scratched behind his ears. "Hey there, Smiley. Good to see you, boy."

"Well, you seem to have a fan," her father said.

"Oh, Smiley just loves Thomas." Annabel bent and gave Smiley a quick kiss on the snout. "Don't you, baby?"

Annabel's mother whirled around and hurried to the house.

Annabel sighed softly and looked at him. "I better see if she needs any help."

He gave her a quick nod and she left.

"So, what's your poison, doc?" Jordyn Leigh, the other sister who still lived at home and was here last Saturday, too, stood at a nearby table holding a bottle of beer in one hand, a pitcher of iced tea in the other.

The beer would've been great, bathing his dry throat with its tangy coldness but Thomas decided to play it safe. Moments later, he found himself sitting with Jazzy and Jordyn Leigh, a glass of iced tea in his hand and Smiley at his side.

Annabel's dad had joined his son at the oversize grill, keeping watch over their dinner as they argued about last night's Colorado Rockies game and the proper way to cook the steaks.

"Will you two knock it off?" a feminine voice called out from behind Thomas. "Jackson, go over there and play referee."

Thomas stood when four more people joined them, assuming the tall blonde and pretty brunette were the last two Cates siblings.

"Hi, Jackson Traub, glad to meet you." A tall man wearing a Stetson held out his hand, his voice laced with a Texas twang. "I'm Laila's husband and it seems the designated arbitrator for this afternoon's festivities."

"Thomas North." He returned the handshake, liking Jackson's easygoing manner. "And is that really necessary?"

"In this family, you bet. I'm Laila," his wife said, taking Thomas's hand next after handing off a foil-covered bowl to one of her sisters. "It's nice to finally meet the man who's been making my little sister even more bubbly than usual."

"We're all your little sisters," the woman standing beside her said. "Even if Annabel has the market cornered on bubbly. Hi there, Thomas," Abby said. "This is my husband, Cade Pritchett."

Thomas shook her hand first and then her husband's. "Nice to meet you, Cade."

"You're looking a little shell-shocked, North." Jackson Traub grabbed a beer from a nearby ice bucket as his wife and Abby moved away to fuss over the food table. "I remember the feeling well."

Thomas was surprised by the frank assessment. "Is it that obvious?"

"Only to someone who was in your shoes this time last year." The man headed for the barbecue, but then turned back. "Hey, thanks for all you've done for my cousin. The entire family appreciates the surgery you did on Forrest."

"I haven't heard from him in a while. Hope things are going well."

"Me, too," Jackson replied, his voice a bit cryptic as he joined the men grill-side.

Soon the three were debating loudly the finer points of cooking over an open fire, with both an oversize spatula and tongs being used for emphasis.

"Come on, doc," Cade said, grabbing a beer for himself. "We should probably join them. Just in case medical attention is needed."

Thomas took his iced tea with him just so he'd have something to do with his hands, and walked across the patio with Cade.

Minutes later, the noise level grew as the conversation switched from cooking to the current standings of their favorites baseball teams. Jackson was the lone holdout with his assurance of the Texas Rangers being play-off bound, but his opinion was voted down so boisterously that Thomas decided just to keep his mouth shut where his Dodgers were concerned.

The men shot statistics and scores back and forth until finally Jackson bet a prized saddle against one of Zeke's horses on the outcome of the World Series.

"I won't hesitate to take that beauty off your hands," Zeke said. "Doesn't matter if you're married to my daughter or not."

"And I'm looking forward to adding that stallion to my growing collection," Jackson shot back. "In fact, I might take him out for a run after dinner. Thomas, do you ride?"

Surprised at the question, Thomas glanced quickly at the feet of all four men. All wore cowboy boots that looked well loved and lived in. Not quite the same as his Italian leather loafers.

"Ah, I haven't in a while," he finally said, realizing he still hadn't answered the question. "Not since my days at boarding school."

Silence filled the air for a moment before Evelyn called out, asking for the status on the meat as everything else was ready. Thomas stepped back as the men all turned to the grill and in fluid movements that showed they'd worked together before, quickly gathered the food that was fully cooked.

Soon everyone was seated around the largest

table; a radio perched nearby was tuned to the local country-music station. After shooing Smiley out of the way, Annabel patted a chair next to her for Thomas to take, handing him a plastic plate and a matching set of silverware. Platters of meat and bowls of salads were passed around and he was encouraged to take whatever he wanted as arms reached back and forth across the table.

Someone spilled a drink, good-natured insults followed and a couple of flying pretzels joined in the mix. The banter flowed from sports to the economy to politics. Everyone talked at once, speaking over each other with no one afraid to voice their opinion no matter what the topic.

Thomas didn't know what to make of it all.

His childhood family dinners had been made up of classical music playing softly in the background, artfully arranged food served on the finest china and dinner conversation with one person speaking at a time. Even now when he dined with his parents and grandmother the evenings were exactly the same.

This…this was chaos.

"Hey, we're going to pull together a game of flag football after dinner," Brody said, elbowing Thomas from where he sat on the other side of him. "You want to join us?"

"Somehow I don't think rolling around in the grass chasing a leather-covered ball is something

Thomas would be interested in," Jazzy said, with a wink.

"Do you like football, Thomas?" Jordyn Leigh asked. "I warn you, it's pretty much a prerequisite to joining the family."

"No, it's not," Annabel protested. "Besides, his favorite team is the Broncos."

"Is that right?" Zeke asked, his eyes bright.

Thomas nodded, feeling as if he'd finally scored points with the man. "Yes, sir."

"Hey, do you feel that?" Cade lifted his beer in a mock salute. "I think the balance of power has shifted ever so slightly."

"What are you talking about?" Laila and Abby asked in unison.

"There's always been six women sitting around the Cates family table, but now we're up to five men." Cade leaned over and clinked his bottle against his father-in-law's. "All we need now is to get your last two daughters married off and the majority power will be all male."

"Amen to that," Zeke offered with a wide smile.

Laughter, jeers and catcalls filled the air but all Thomas felt was the rising panic at how everyone at the table already had him walking down the aisle while Annabel said nothing to ebb their train of thought.

Suddenly, he couldn't breathe, his chest and throat tight. The need to escape was so overwhelming Thomas almost missed the ringing of his cell phone. He reached for it, trying to ignore the hard lump in his gut, and peered at the display.

"I need to answer this," he gasped in Annabel's ear. "Is there somewhere I can go that's a bit quieter?"

"Of course." She wiped her hands and rose to her feet.

Thomas did the same and addressed the table. "Please excuse me. I need to make a call to the hospital."

The lively talking paused for a moment, then started back up as they walked away, diminishing slightly as they entered the cool interior of the house.

Annabel waved him into the kitchen, but stayed by the door as he walked farther away and hit the button that would connect him directly to TC General. As he listened to the call, the lump in his gut grew.

Damn, not the news he was hoping for.

After a few minutes he ended the call and walked back to her. "I'm sorry. I have to leave."

"What's wrong?"

He paused, weighing exactly what he should say. "It's Maurice Owens."

"Oh!" Her eyes filled with concern. "That poor, sweet man. Is it bad?"

Thomas knew Annabel had come to care for his patient over the past week, often stopping in to see the old man even without Smiley, but he couldn't go into the details with her. "Serious enough that I need to say my goodbyes and get to the hospital right away."

They went back outside. Thomas explained he'd had an emergency come up and offered his apologies for having to leave early. He returned her father's handshake, thanking the man for having him in his home and again read concern in her mother's eyes when Annabel grabbed his hand and insisted on walking him to his car.

"Will you call me later?" she asked and hurried to keep up with his quick strides. "I'd like to know how Maurice is doing."

Thomas glanced at his watch as he opened the driver's side door. It was after six already. "I don't have any idea how late that might be."

"I'll be up." She leaned in and gave him a quick kiss. "I can come over, too, you know, later on. If you need me."

He didn't know if it was her offer or the heat of her lips on his that caused that hard lump in his gut to rise up to his throat.

Unable to spare the time to figure out which the correct answer was, he shoved the thought from his head and slid behind the wheel. His focus right now had to be solely on his patient. "I can't make any promises."

"I know that, I was just…" Her voice trailed off as she stepped away from the car. "Please drive safe."

Eight hours later, Thomas finally dragged his tired self inside his home. Alone. It was after two in the morning and he was dead on his feet.

Maurice Owens had suffered a series of seizures and they were still trying to find the cause. The last one had been so strong they had no choice but to place the man in a medically induced coma to prevent brain damage.

The elderly gentleman had been doing so well ever since Smiley had started to visit, his recovery progressing much faster than estimated that Thomas had almost been willing to admit—

No. He shut down that thought, refusing to go there.

Not now. Not tonight.

Thomas had sat in his office for the past two hours going over the man's medical records and test results, certain that he'd missed something. A leg with multiple fractures wasn't good for anyone, least of all a man who was close to celebrating his one hundredth birthday. And the chances of someone Maurice's age not suffering any additional side effects from the seizures or the coma were slim at best.

Eyes glazed over and a headache on the edge of erupting, Thomas had finally noticed the time. Realizing he'd never called Annabel, he decided to head home. His place was so quiet after the craziness at Annabel's and the constant noise of the hospital. The silence seeped into his bones and he realized just how tired he was.

Heading upstairs, he toed off his shoes and socks and stripped off his shirt. He undid his belt and yanked down the zipper on his pants, pausing when his gaze landed on the multicolored quilt folded neatly over the back of a chair in the corner of his bedroom.

It was the same quilt he'd found in his living room the morning after they'd made love the first time. Annabel had brought it back with her last night, insisting he keep it as the blanket's muted shades fit perfectly in his home's color scheme.

Besides, she'd said, she was always cold, despite the warm summer night, and they'd cuddled beneath the quilt until soon the soft material was the only thing protecting their bare skin from the cool air-conditioning.

Thomas grabbed the blanket off the chair, brought it to his face, and breathed deeply. Annabel's scent filled his head, but soon memories of this afternoon and tonight did, as well.

Her family's comments linking him and Annabel, the sight of Maurice's body flailing uncontrollably, the soft blue eyes offering to come to him when he called, the aged, unseeing gaze, clouded with confusion, pain and then no expression at all....

Thomas still didn't know what he missed when it came to his patient's health, but he knew one thing.

If he hadn't been spending so much time over the past three days with Annabel, thinking about her when they weren't together, and anticipating when he was going to see her again, he would have seen this coming. He should have known his patient was heading down the wrong path, a path that could take the man's life.

Tossing the blanket down, Thomas turned and headed for his bed, ignoring the urge to call Annabel even at this late hour.

He was not going to pick up that phone.

No matter how much he wanted to.

Chapter Eleven

"Please, I need to see him." Annabel leaned over the counter, doing her best to persuade the nurse on duty, who happened to be an old high school friend, to bend the rules just a little bit. "I need to know if he's okay."

After waiting for hours with no phone call from Thomas on Maurice's condition, she'd finally fallen asleep around two this morning. When she'd woken up and still didn't have an update, she'd taken a quick shower and headed for the hospital, determined to find out what was going on.

"I'm sorry, but only family can visit patients in intensive care," Jody replied, her voice a low whisper. "You know that, Annabel."

"Maurice Owens doesn't have any family." A sense of hopelessness weighed heavily on her shoulders. She glanced at her watch, noting she needed to be at the library in forty-five minutes for a mandatory budget meeting. "He's over ninety years old and he's all alone in this world. Smiley and I have been by to visit him a few times last week and I've come by myself even more often. He was doing so much better. I don't understand—"

She broke off when the tears threatened, but pulled in a deep breath instead of letting them overpower her and forced herself to continue. "Jody, please. Can you at least tell me how he'd doing? Why he was moved here from his regular room?"

Jody's fingers flew over the keyboard in front of her for a moment, then her expression changed from stern to surprised. "If you'll follow me, I'll take you to his room."

"You will?" Shock radiated through Annabel. "But how? You just said I couldn't go in."

Her friend smiled as she rose and walked around the desk. "Your name just appeared on the approved visitors list. Believe me, it wasn't there a few minutes ago when you first asked. The attending physician must have made the change. Doctor's orders."

Doctor's orders.

Thomas's orders.

He had to be the one who granted permission for

her to follow the petite nurse through the security doors into the hush of the intensive-care area.

Did he somehow know she was here this morning? Was he here?

The urge to look around and see if he was nearby flowed through her, but she kept her gaze firmly on her friend as they walked down the long corridor.

"Okay, here we are." Jody stopped outside a glass door, her voice a hushed whisper. "All I can tell you is Mr. Owens suffered a series of seizures last night. As far as I know the doctors don't know why yet, but he is currently in a coma in order to keep him stable."

The tears threatened again, but Annabel held them off as she nodded her understanding.

"You only have fifteen minutes until the morning's visiting hours are over," Jody continued. "But you can come back later."

Annabel leaned in and gave her friend a hug. "Thank you, Jody, so much."

Entering the room, Annabel's eyes were drawn right away to the elderly man lying so still in the bed. She walked to a chair next to him and sat down, instinctively reaching out to grasp Maurice's hand. His skin was almost gray in color, wrinkled, and covered with age spots, but until now his grip had been strong whenever she'd held his hand.

"Hey there, Maurice." Annabel's heart ached for her new friend, but she kept her voice light. "Boy, when you said you were ready to get out of that room upstairs I don't think this is what you meant."

She swallowed hard and kept talking. "You know, they'll never allow Smiley to come into the ICU. You're going to have to get better so you two can spend some time together again. You promised to play catch with him, and Smiley just loves to chase a ball...."

Pressing a hand to her mouth as her voice faded, Annabel closed her eyes and offered a quick prayer for this very special man. A man who'd fought valiantly for his country during both the Second World War and the Korean Conflict. A man who often spoke of his wife, who he'd fallen in love with long after he thought his chance at happiness had passed him by, and how much he missed their simple home while being stuck in the hospital.

"You rest and get better, Maurice," she whispered. "I'll be back to see you very soon."

Rising, Annabel released his hand and leaned over to place a light kiss on the elderly man's forehead. After leaving his room, she walked out to the main corridor, her mind once again filled with thoughts of Thomas.

She still didn't know why he hadn't called her last night to give her an update on Maurice's condition. Not even a message on her cell phone. He had to know how worried she'd be...how much she'd wanted to make sure that Maurice was okay.

That he, too, had been okay.

As thankful as she was that he'd added her to Maurice's visitors list this morning, she still had no idea what was going on with Thomas. Deciding there was no time like the present to find out, Annabel quickly took the stairs up to the second floor, her high heels echoing on the polished linoleum as she made her way toward his office.

She had no idea what she would say to him once she got there, but she wasn't worried. The words would come. They always did. Except for yesterday when her family had so easily lumped her and Thomas together.

Heck, the way they'd carried on during the barbecue, they practically had them married!

While she had pleaded with them beforehand to make Thomas feel comfortable and at home, she'd never expected her brothers-in-law to go as far as they did.

As much as she liked the tingling that filled her bones at the idea of someday being Mrs. Thomas North, she'd known she needed to say something to downplay their teasing. Something along the lines of how she and Thomas had only been on a few dates, while leaving out the part about the great sex over the past three days for her parents' sake.

She'd been about to do just that when Thomas had gotten the call that forced him to leave early.

And yes, he did seem intently focused on Maurice

when he'd left, but she was smart enough to pick up that a small part of him was relieved to be out of the line of fire where her family was concern.

Not that she blamed him, because despite how easily the subject matter had changed from the two of them to something else once he'd left, she had to put up with the "I told you so" look and a few underhanded remarks from her mother about what life would be like married to a doctor.

Not that any of that excused him from not calling and letting her know about Maurice.

Confusion swamped her as she entered his office area, surprised to find both Marge's desk and Thomas's inner office empty. From the half-empty mug of coffee and paperwork scattered across his desk, she could tell he'd arrived already, he just wasn't here.

She checked her watch again and then grabbed a small pad of paper, determined to leave him a quick note. Three tries, three crumpled balls of paper later and she still didn't know what to say.

Why didn't you call?

I miss you.

When will we see each other again?

Oh, all of those openings seemed so...so...desperate? And Annabel didn't want him to think of her that way.

Yes, she was in love.

Yes, he was the one for her.

Two amazing and wonderful facts she'd carried in

her heart since the first time they'd made love. But she wanted Thomas to come to those same conclusions on his own, in his own way and time.

Deciding it was best to just call his office later and speak to him in person, she tossed the pad back onto Thomas's desk and headed for the doorway when voices from the outer office stopped her.

"And who would've thought the guy had enough time on his hands to steal my wife."

What?

Annabel's hand stilled on the door knob. Instead of moving to the other side of the door, she stood there, frozen.

"I mean, we've only been married a year," the man continued. "Aren't we supposed to still be in some damn honeymoon phase?"

"That's rough. Sorry you're going through all that."

Okay, that voice she recognized as Thomas's. The other man must be a friend of his.

"You know, people warned me about getting married during my residency, but we'd been together since college. I loved her. I thought she loved me," the friend went on. "Then I find out she's been spending time with some hot-shot lawyer while I'm busting my ass working long shifts here." The man sighed. "Sorry I'm unloading my problems on you."

Annabel's heart ached for the poor guy's obvious pain over his wife's infidelity. She should make her presence known, but the last thing she wanted was to embarrass the man, or Thomas. Better to step back and give them as much privacy as—

"I understand it's tough, but you can't let your personal life get in the way of your work here. That minor slip you had earlier with your patient could have become a major issue, if you hadn't caught it in time." Thomas's voice was low, but strong and filled with certainty. "Love and medicine don't mix. I found that out the hard way."

His last statements stunned her and Annabel found it impossible to move.

"Look, I'm the last person who should give out advice on something like this," Thomas continued.

"No, please," his friend pushed. "I want your opinion."

Silence filled the air for a long moment and Annabel found herself holding her breath waiting to see how Thomas would respond.

"I've learned that being one hundred percent committed to your career is a prerequisite for our profession. Anything less and people's lives are at stake," he finally said. "Some can find a balance between a personal life and a professional one, some can't. You need to find out which group you belong to."

"Have *you* figured that out yet?"

She pressed a hand to her mouth to stop herself from blurting out how wrong he was, how finding a balance was a part of being in love no matter what someone's line of work. Annabel closed her eyes, her heart pounding in her chest as she waited for Thomas to answer.

"All I know is you have to weigh the facts against the evidence. In my experience, trusting in love is crazy and I— Ah, hello, Marge."

Thomas cut off his words as his secretary arrived, ending the men's discussion. Turning away, Annabel walked to the windows, brushing away the tears before they could fall. She wrapped her arms tightly around herself, suddenly very cold despite the suit jacket she wore.

Wishing a hole in the floor would open up and swallow her would do no good. All she could do was wait and—what?

Hope that Thomas and Marge left again so she could sneak out unseen? Where would that leave her?

Still waiting for Thomas to come to her?

No, what she needed was to make a few things clear to him. At least one thing in particular. She knew what was in her heart and now seemed like the perfect time to share—

"Annabel?"

She whirled around.

"What are you—" Thomas stood in his doorway, shock on his face. He quickly glanced back out at the outer office before closing the door behind him. "How long have you been in here?"

"Long enough. I'm sorry. I didn't mean to eavesdrop." She waved one hand toward his desk. "I stopped by to see you, but you were gone. I was going to leave a note. Then I heard... I didn't want to interrupt a private conversation."

"So you just listened instead?"

"It was pretty hard not to. Oh, Thomas, I can't believe you really feel that way about love."

He moved to the other side of his desk, his attention on the paperwork in his hand. "Now is not the time to talk about this."

"I think this is the perfect time." Annabel reached deep inside for that certainty she'd been so sure of just a moment ago. "Thomas, I—"

"I'm guessing you came here to check on Maurice," he interrupted her. "I didn't call you last night because it was late when I finally got home. Actually it was very early this morning." Thomas dropped the folder to his desk. "I can't go into any detail about my patient's care—"

"I know he's in intensive care and I know I have you to thank for allowing me to see him." Annabel waved off his explanation, determined not to let him pull away from what they really needed to talk about. "Thank you for that. I'm sure you and the rest of the staff are doing all you can for him."

His gaze remained focused on his desk. "Yes, we are."

Annabel remained silent, but when he didn't say anything more, she purposely walked to him, invading his personal space as she slid between him and his desk.

He tried to step back, pushing his chair to one side, but the credenza behind him stopped him.

"Do you really believe it's crazy to trust in love?"

Thomas purposely kept his gaze away from her. "Annabel…"

"I don't, and do you want to know why?" She placed her fingertips at his jaw and gently forced him to look at her. "Because I love you, Thomas."

He closed his eyes and pressed his mouth into a hard line before he spoke. "No, you don't."

Yes, she did. Saying the words aloud for the first time made her even more certain of her feelings for this man.

"Yes, I do."

He opened his eyes again, the glacial chill in their blue depths surprising her. "You can't know that."

"Of course I can and I wanted you to know." Undeterred, she dropped her hand to his chest, the steady beat of his heart beneath her fingers reminding her of those nights when he'd held her close. "This may seem a bit sudden considering—"

"Sudden?" Thomas turned away from her, moving out from behind his desk. "Yes, I would say so. We've only known each other a couple of weeks."

"I'm sure of my feelings, Thomas, but knowing that I love you doesn't mean I have the future all planned out." Pushing aside the panic that the distance he was putting between them was more than physical, Annabel followed him. "Goodness knows, I'm very much a live-in-the-moment kind of person, but what I'm certain of is that I want you in every one of those moments."

"After such a short period of time?" The disbelief was evident in his voice as he crossed his office; this time he was the one staring out the windows. "How is that possible?"

"I don't know how." She wanted to reach out, to make him turn and look at her, but the stiffness of his posture held her back. "I just know that what we have is special and worth all the craziness that might come our way as we muddle through this."

"Worth it to whom? My patients? I can't allow my personal life to get in the way. To distract me from…" Thomas's voice trailed off as he pinched the bridge of his nose hard and sighed.

"Is that what you think?" Annabel quickly connected the dots. "That because you and I have been spending time together over the past few days you missed something in Maurice's treatment—"

"It doesn't matter what I think." Thomas spun around. "What I rely on are facts, while you place all of your trust in your feelings."

"Yes, I guess I do. And from what I overheard, you've been hurt in the past, but please don't let that affect what's happening now between us. You must know what we have is wonderful..."

"What I know is that I have a lot of work to do." Thomas's gaze traveled the length of her. "And you look like you're on your way to an important meeting."

Annabel glanced down at her business suit. "Yes," she finally admitted. "I need to get to the library."

"Well, please don't let me keep you."

The distance on his face spoke volumes at how far apart they were despite standing right in front of each other. For the first time, the words wouldn't come and Annabel had no idea how to reach him.

"I'm free tonight." She pushed the invitation past her lips, already knowing deep inside the reception her words would receive. "If you want to get together?"

"I'll probably be working late again." Thomas grabbed a white medical coat off a nearby hook. Sliding it over his shoulders, he pulled it on like a suit of body armor, leaving Annabel standing there alone and defenseless.

"Thomas, I—"

"Annabel, please." He started to reach for her, but curled his fingers into a tight fist and jammed it into his pocket. "I can't talk about this right now, and I really need to get back to work."

Pressing her palm hard against her chest as if she

could actually stop her heart from breaking, Annabel could only nod before she turned and walked away, certain that this time he wouldn't be coming after her.

Chapter Twelve

It amazed Thomas how much life could change in a mere seventy-two hours.

On Monday morning he had no clue as to the reason for Maurice Owens's seizures. Today the man was scheduled to be released from intensive care. They'd finally determined a blood infection was the source of the problems. After a heavy dose of IV antibiotics, the man now fully awake, alert and, according to his nurses, asking when that rag mop of a dog and his pretty owner were coming back to see him.

Annabel and Smiley.

Thomas's fist tightened on the bag he carried as he crossed the parking lot and headed inside the hospital.

Yeah, life had certainly changed since that Monday morning when he'd done the one thing he'd wanted to avoid from the moment he'd met Annabel.

Hurt her.

After he'd made it clear he didn't believe her declaration, the pain and disappointment in her eyes before she'd turned and walked out of his office had filled him with such remorse he'd actually started after her. Then common sense took over. Even so, stopping himself from chasing after her had taken every ounce of strength he had.

Let her go. Let her go. Let her go.

The words had echoed in his head, a resounding anthem that told him he'd done the right thing.

He hadn't seen her since.

His daily rounds and Maurice's unstable condition had kept him occupied for the next twenty-four hours until his boss ordered him to go home and not return until he'd gotten some much-needed rest. He'd obeyed and fell into a dreamless sleep for over fifteen hours, woke long enough to choke down some food, check in with Marge and then slept again.

But this time he'd dreamed of Annabel.

Her looking at him smiling and happy, her beautiful blue eyes filled with joy as she chatted about her work at the library, the therapy dog program, her family.

But then the joy faded, replaced with the same bewilderment and hurt that *he'd* put there as she faded farther and farther from his outstretched hands until she disappeared in swirling mist....

He'd shot awake, drenched in sweat and tangled in the sheets of his empty bed, his heart pounding in his chest. The urge to call her, to hear her voice, had been so powerful he'd grabbed his phone and held it in a grip so tight his knuckles ached.

But he couldn't do it. He couldn't put her through that again.

She'd laid her heart in his hands, and he'd all but thrown it back at her. He hadn't believed her when she poured out her feelings about how she felt about him, about *them*.

He couldn't do it because he hadn't changed his mind.

No matter how hollow and empty he might feel at the moment, making the choice of his patients over a personal life had been the right one.

He meant what he'd said to the young resident on his staff. Some in their profession managed to balance both a career and a life outside of the hospital, but others, the majority, tried and failed.

The consequences could be much worse than a broken heart.

He couldn't take that chance.

After his shower this morning, he'd dressed and started to leave his bedroom when the quilt Annabel had given him caught his attention.

He'd reached for it, ignoring how his fingers

shook as he grabbed the soft material. Marching downstairs and into the kitchen, he quickly stuffed the blanket into a paper sack.

Returning the gift was a necessity for the both of them.

Annabel had her Thursday session with Smiley this afternoon at the hospital. He was certain she would be there, just like she'd been every day this week visiting with Maurice, her name scrawled on the visitors' log in her loopy handwriting, which made his chest hurt every time he saw it.

He didn't have any idea what he was going to say when he came face-to-face with her, but he would think of something over the next six hours.

Even if it was only goodbye.

Exiting the elevator, he walked down the hall to his office and had to swallow the hard lump in his throat before he greeted Marge, who sat at her desk, the phone receiver in her hand.

"Morning, Marge."

"Oh, Dr. North." She looked up at him, surprise in her eyes. "I'm glad you're here. I was just about to page you."

He disregarded the natural quickening of his pulse. "What is it?"

"Mr. Owens is being a bit cantankerous this morning." She placed the receiver back in its cradle. "The head nurse in ICU just called to say he's insisting on seeing you *before* they move him."

Thomas dropped his briefcase and the bag into the closest chair. "I'll go right now. Can you please put these in my office?"

"That's quite a big lunch you're brown bagging today."

Turning to grab some much-needed coffee, he snapped a lid on the disposable cup and kept his gaze from returning to the bag. "That's not food."

"Is it something I can take care of for you?"

For a split second Thomas almost agreed to Marge's request. He could easily ask her to take it down to the session or even mail it to Annabel at her home, but he quickly squashed the idea. "No."

He softened his tone when the woman offered him a raised eyebrow. "Thank you, but that's something…it's something I need to handle on my own."

Three hours later Thomas returned to his office.

He'd gone ahead and completed his morning rounds after making sure Maurice was settled in his new room, which wasn't the same one he'd been in before. A fact the elderly man found very unsettling until Thomas had promised him the staff would make sure the new room number was available for anyone who asked for it.

Anyone meaning Annabel.

He hated to admit it, but he'd been disappointed to find out she hadn't made it in yet to see Maurice this morning unlike the past two days when she'd come by during the early visiting hours.

Another reason Maurice had been upset.

Thomas met up with Marge in the hallway just as she was leaving. "On your way out for lunch?"

"Yes, I need to pick up my cats from the vet." She pulled her keys from her purse. "They went in this morning for their checkups and the poor things hate it there. I want to get them home as soon as possible."

He peeked at her desk, noting the bag and his briefcase were gone, but he asked anyway, gesturing toward the still-closed door to his inner office. "Did you put my things inside?"

"I started to, but she insisted on taking that beautiful quilt into your office herself."

He stilled, his feet suddenly rooted to the floor. "She?"

"The bag tipped over when she bumped the chair and we couldn't help but see what was inside," Marge called out over her shoulder as she kept walking. "I tried to put it back, but she insisted and I knew it was useless to argue. Oh, and she was also adamant about waiting for you, too. Be back soon."

Before Thomas could say another word, Marge disappeared with a quick wave.

He remained standing there, staring at the door, trying to grasp the fact that Annabel was waiting for him on the other side.

Her coming back here to his office was the last thing he'd planned on, the last thing he expected. It was too early for Smiley's session. She must have come to see Maurice.

And him.

He pulled in a deep breath and moved forward, regretting that he didn't have the afternoon to figure out exactly what he was going to say to her. That he'd brought the quilt to the hospital was probably explanation enough, but still she'd persisted on waiting for him.

Determined to keep his focus completely on the facts and not the wild beating of his heart, he straightened his tie, turned the latch and stepped inside. His gaze was immediately drawn to the woman sitting at one end of his couch, the quilt spread over her lap, her fingertips tracing the mutely shaded blocks and the intricate stitching.

"Grandmother?"

Ernestine's hand stilled as she raised her head. "Good morning, Thomas. Or should I say good afternoon. You know, this quilt is a beautiful piece of work."

He walked farther into the room, bombarded with regret when he realized it wasn't Annabel who was waiting for him.

He tried to control the emotional roller coaster he was riding, knowing the fact he was on this ride in the first place was of his own doing. "Ah, yes, it is."

"The time and attention to detail it took to create such a lovely work of art." She returned her attention to the quilt, her hands again moving lightly over the fabric. "Someone must have been working on this for a very long time."

"Almost two years."

The words left his mouth before he'd even realized he spoke, remembering Annabel telling him about how she'd started the quilt as a way to keep busy during a crazy winter storm that dumped almost two feet of snow on Thunder Canyon.

He'd spent that same long weekend holed up in his empty condo with nothing but a home designer's catalog to flip through. It still amazed him how the colors she'd chosen had perfectly matched the furniture, carpeting and drapes he'd picked for his place that first weekend he'd been back in town.

Deciding he'd better sit before his shaky legs gave out on him, Thomas moved to the chair behind his desk.

"And it fits so perfectly with both your office and your home. Wherever did you have it made?"

"I didn't. I mean, it wasn't created specifically for me. For my place. The fact it matches is…just a fluke."

"Oh?" His grandmother slightly tilted her head, a familiar motion that spoke volumes despite her abbreviated question.

"It was a gift, actually." He paused and cleared his suddenly tight throat. "An unplanned gift. From a friend."

That caused his grandmother's gaze to sharpen with curiosity. "A lady friend?"

Thomas remained silent.

"A very special lady friend." Her words were spoken as a statement of fact as she answered her own question. "Well, that's even better."

"No, it's not."

She laced her fingers together and rested them primly on her quilt-covered lap. "I'm intrigued. Please go on."

"There is nothing to be intrigued about, Grandmother." He leaned back in his chair, forcing himself to appear relaxed as he returned her direct stare. "There is no special lady friend."

"But there was."

A heartbeat passed. "Yes, but it's over."

This time her head tilted ever so slightly in the opposite direction. "And does Miss Cates share in that assessment of your relationship?"

Thomas couldn't contain his shock. "How did— How did you know it was Annabel Cates?"

"Oh, my darling, you'd be surprised at the things I know." Ernestine gently folded the quilt into a neat package and laid it next to her on the couch. "With age comes wisdom, as the saying goes."

"What exactly does that mean?"

"It means I was hoping you would find more here in Thunder Canyon than just a brilliant career that you've worked so hard for and deservedly so."

Then it hit Thomas that his grandmother knew everything that happened back in California. "How did you find out?"

"Haven't you learned by now that there's little that goes on in this hospital that I don't know about? Including the professional backgrounds of our staff?" She held up a hand when he started to speak. "And when one of those staff members is related to me you can be certain my fellow administrators made sure I was aware of what exactly led to you looking for work away from Santa Monica."

Thomas leaned forward, bracing his elbows on his knees. "I'm sorry. I should've told you about all of that myself—"

"No apologies necessary, Thomas." She cut him off. "The way your personal and professional lives collided, and the fallout it created, was not something you could control."

"It was my fault."

"You were lied to. Your feelings were manipulated. How can you take responsibility for that?"

"I have to." Thomas rose and walked to the window, unable to take the sympathy he saw in his grandmother's eyes. "I have to make sure that 'collision,' as you called it, never happens again."

"By closing off your heart?"

"By choosing to focus all of my attention on my patients." Despite the rudeness of the gesture, he kept his back to her. "I missed something last weekend that could've cost a man his life."

"But it didn't."

"No, but to take that chance again…" He turned and looked at his grandmother. Pride welling inside him at all she'd accomplished here at the hospital, at what his family has achieved in this town. "To do anything that would result in a repeat of what happened in the past, to bring shame to this hospital, our family…to you. I won't take that risk."

"Thomas—"

"Besides, love and marriage and medicine aren't a good mix. Look at all the people here at TC General going through breakups and divorces."

His grandmother smiled as she stood, using her cane for balance as she walked toward him. "Thomas, you could say the same thing about any profession. Love and marriage take a lot of hard work, commitment and attention to keep it strong and healthy, just like any career does."

"Mother and Father haven't had to work that hard."

"Yes, they have," she countered. "Children don't always see all that goes into their parents' relationship, especially you because you were away so often at school and such. Believe me, with the two of them being hardheaded lawyers, like your grandpa Joe, they made some of their arguments more entertaining than most federal court cases."

His grandmother's assessment of his parents' stable and rather sedate marriage surprised him. Even more so was the hint that her own marriage had suffered its share of ups and downs. "You and Grandpa Joe?"

"We had our troubles as well, darling." She reached out and laid a hand on his arm. "Both long before and after that horrible accident. When we first met, your grandfather told me on our third date that we were going to spend the rest of our lives together. To an eighteen-year-old girl that sounded crazy, but he was so sure we were meant to be together."

Thomas did the math quickly in his head. "But you were married just before your nineteenth birthday."

"Yes, we were. With a lot of promises of forever from him and a big leap of faith on my part." Her eyes filled with long-ago memories. "Your grandfather told me he loved me enough for the both of us and that would carry us through until I was sure. And he was right. When he lost his legs all those years later, it was my turn to be the one to convince him our love was strong enough, that I could be strong enough, for the both of us."

"But you'd been married over three decades when that happened." Thomas remembered his own devastation at what his grandfather had suffered through when Thomas was a child. To picture those events again from his grandmother's point of view put a totally new spin on things. "Looking back now, as an adult and a doctor, I can see all he had to deal with, both physically and mentally, but I honestly never thought your marriage—"

"Our marriage lasted another twenty years because we found a way to make our love strong again, a feat achieved many times over." Her attention was back fully on him. "The ups and downs, the good times and bad, the strengths and weaknesses…when you find the right person, when you're that lucky, you need to grab ahold of that love and never let go. Fifty-five years or fifty-five days…I would've been happy with either because I was with the man I loved."

Thomas turned back to stare out the window again, folding his arms over his chest after his grandmother released her hold on him. His head swirled with everything she'd said, making sorting it into logical steps and facts difficult.

Falling back on his training, he started compartmentalizing, pushing away his emotions even as the desire to find Annabel, to go to her, surged inside of him.

The gentle cuff to the back of his head caught him completely by surprise.

He turned to stare at his grandmother, his mouth rising into a grin that matched hers. It'd been years since she'd swatted him one.

"What was that for?"

"I know you're going to think and reason and debate all we've talked about, because that's who you are and that's what you do, but don't take too long." She turned and headed for the door. "Your young lady doesn't seem to be as naive as I once was. I think it might take a lot more than fancy words and heartfelt promises to show her how wrong you were."

"I didn't say I was wrong."

"Not yet, you haven't." She glanced back and gave him a quick wink. "You're a smart boy. You'll get there eventually."

Thomas turned back to the window after his grandmother departed, closing the door behind her.

He didn't know how long he stood there, reflecting on the past few days, weeks and years. Thinking about all he'd gone through in California thanks to both his own choices and the things that had been out of his control.

Yes, he'd fallen hard and fast for Victoria and he'd overlooked—or just didn't want to see—the obvious signs that something was wrong with their relationship from the start. All the hiding and secrecy over the months they'd spent together should've been red flags that everything wasn't as it seemed.

She wasn't all she seemed.

While his day-to-day work at the hospital hadn't been affected, his career had suffered because of his own actions, even more so, by all that Victoria had done. Not just to him but to the poor schmuck still married to her.

Annabel wasn't Victoria though.

Yes, they'd only known each other a few weeks, but the way he felt when he was with her was so much more than he'd ever experienced with Victoria. With anyone, for that matter.

And the only one trying to keep their crazy and wonderful courtship a secret had been him, because of the past.

When he'd finally admitted to himself—and to her—how much he wanted her, wanted to be with her, everything fell in place so easily. It was almost scary at how perfect they fit.

Another reason why he'd tried to run.

Not that everything would always fit so flawlessly. They came from two different worlds. Her loud and adoring family, so different from his small and demure one, would require some getting used to. His demanding career, her devotion to her dog and their equally strong commitment to both would also require a lot of give and take.

The bottom line?

Finding a way to bring his world and hers together would be challenging and fun and well worth the effort.

Thomas moved back to his desk and sat, thinking about everything his grandmother had said about the hard work and commitment that came with making a relationship last.

He kept coming to the same conclusion.

Why was he running away from the best thing that ever happened to him? Fighting his feelings, hiding from them was useless because they weren't going to change.

Not now. Not ever.

But what to do to show that he'd finally understood? That he was finally sure?

The idea came to him quickly and while it might be a small first step, it was an important one.

He quickly booted up his computer, typed a simple request in the search engine and waited. As soon as the website appeared he scanned the images, one after the other, until he found the perfect one. Blonde, bubbly and a face that showed all the love in the world to give.

With one click he checked his calendar, relieved to find it empty for the afternoon. Rising, he rounded his desk and headed for the door.

"I'm out of here for the day, Marge," he said to his secretary, glad to see she'd returned. "I'll have my cell phone on if any emergencies arise."

"Has your grandmother left?" she asked.

"Yes, she did." He didn't even slow down as he hurried past her desk.

"Where are you going?" she called after him.

"To see a woman about a dog."

Chapter Thirteen

Forcing a smile had never been something Annabel needed to do, but today, despite stopping in and finding Maurice sleeping comfortably in his new room, it took all the energy she had to remain positive during this afternoon's Smiley session.

She'd left behind a note and an arrangement of brightly colored daisies for Maurice to find when he awoke, ushering Smiley away from the bed after he'd nudged at the sleeping man's hand.

Once they arrived at the therapy area, they'd found a roomful of patients already waiting, with more coming and going as the two hours passed. Annabel had already contacted a few members of her therapy group with the idea of adding more dogs to this weekly open session. Having two or three additional animals would allow each person to have more one-on-one time as many were often reluctant to allow Smiley to move on.

Of course, she still needed to get approval from— Thomas.

Still on bended knee, Smiley at her side after they'd said goodbye to the last child, Annabel bowed her head, blinking hard against the endless supply of tears.

Would they ever stop?

After the past three days one would think she'd exhausted her supply. But after Annabel had responded to her mother's innocently asked "how was your day" on Monday night by bursting into wrenching sobs, her mother had lovingly pointed out to her that the tears would end when the healing began.

Annabel wasn't sure that would ever happen.

Something deep inside told her that while the crippling ache in her heart might one day ease, the empty space left behind would always belong to the one man she'd been so sure was the love of her life.

A man who couldn't—wouldn't—accept her love.

Smiley's snout nuzzled her shoulder, his nose cool against her neck. Annabel sighed and her pet moved even closer, instinctively knowing how much his owner needed his faithful and unconditional love.

"Thank you, sweetie." Annabel wrapped her arms

around the dog's shoulders and gave him a gentle hug. Smiley had rarely left her side since greeting her at the door on Monday. "I don't know how I'd get through all of this without you."

"I was just thinking the same thing."

The low masculine voice caused Annabel to look up.

Shock filled her at the sight of Forrest Traub standing in front of her. Rising, she brushed the tears off her cheeks. "What are *you* doing here?"

The tall man leaned heavily on his cane as he held out one hand for her dog to inspect. "I'm here to see you. And Smiley."

Seconds later, Smiley offered a quick lick to the man's fingers and was rewarded with a firm scratch behind his ears.

Forrest leaned over and spoke gently to her pet. Annabel silently thanked him, sure he'd seen her crying, and used those few moments to pull in and then release a deep shuddering breath.

She had no idea why Forrest Traub was back in town or why he'd come looking for her. "No, what I meant was what are you doing back in Thunder Canyon? I was told you'd returned to your family's ranch."

"I did, for a while." Forrest straightened. "But my brother Clay and I have decided to move to Thunder Canyon on a permanent basis."

Her gaze flickered for a moment to his leg and

the brace still visible beneath his faded jeans. "For your treatment?"

His grip again tightened on the curved handle of his cane. "Among other reasons."

"Ah. Would you like to sit?" Annabel waved at a pair of nearby chairs, already inching toward the one farthest away. "Smiley's session ended a few minutes ago, but I don't think they'll kick us out just yet."

Forrest sank into the chair, his injured leg stretched out in front of him. Smiley moved in, placing his chin immediately on the man's good knee, just like he'd done that first day.

"I've been standing in the corner for the last few minutes, watching you work," Forrest said, his lips rising into a small grin when Smiley lifted his head and looked up at him. "Watching both of you work. I'd heard from my cousin about how popular your sessions have become. I guess you were able to convince Dr. North to give your idea a go."

Annabel ignored the kick to her gut at the memory of how she and Thomas first met, just a few short weeks ago. "Yes, I did."

"Do you have any interest in expanding them?"

Pushing aside her heartache, Annabel was happy for the distraction and equally surprised at how Forrest's question echoed her own thoughts from a moment ago. "I have been thinking of bringing in more dogs to spread the attention around."

"My idea is different."

"What's that?"

"I'd like to start a support group just for veterans."

Annabel thought back to the two servicemen, both recently returned from Afghanistan, who'd come to the first private session she held on Tuesdays. Despite the small size of the group, neither had been back since even though both were still patients here in the hospital.

They'd admitted to being strangers to one another during introductions, but had instinctively sat next to each other that first time. The chairs had formed a large circle, but the two men had remained emotionally, if not physically, separated from the other patients, both choosing not to speak, even during their turn with Smiley.

"That's an interesting idea," she said, watching as Forrest finally reached out and began scratching Smiley's ears again. "What made you think of it?"

Silence filled the room. Annabel waited, hoping he would share his inspiration when he was ready.

"I often thought about Smiley over the last few weeks. Just that short amount of time I spent with him really had an impact on me." Forrest kept his focus on her pet as he talked. "Being back on the ranch was harder than I'd thought it'd be. I honestly don't think I would've gone down to the barn to see the horses I still can't ride if I hadn't felt—if Smiley hadn't made me realize how much I missed…"

Annabel remained silent, watching the array of

emotions that crossed the man's handsome features. It was almost as if she could see his attempts at gathering his thoughts after his voice had faded with his last words.

"Animals offer an unrestricted love, don't they?" he finally said, his attention still focused on the repeated motion of his hand moving easily over Smiley's fur. "No questions, no divided loyalties, no demands or restrictions."

Everything Forrest said resounded deeply inside Annabel and made all her hard work with Smiley worthwhile. "You've obviously thought a lot about this."

"I haven't had much to do with my time lately but think."

"And heal," Annabel added.

Forrest lifted one shoulder in a shrug. "Physically, maybe, although that's taking longer than everyone, including myself, ever thought it would. But it's what's going on inside, the learning to let go of…certain behaviors, certain memories, that I think Smiley could help with. Not just for me, but others who have served their country, as well."

She could easily understand how letting go or at least learning to live with the memories of serving in a war might be difficult. From the straightforward hurting of being away from their loved ones to the unimaginable horror of living day to day, moment to moment, in a place where each decision could mean life or death, these men and women had been to hell and back.

"What do you mean by certain behaviors?" she questioned. "If you don't mind me asking."

"Soldiers tend to keep their problems to themselves. It isn't easy for them to rely on other people." Forrest's voice was low, his gaze now focused straight ahead at the large expanse of windows across the room. "Even the men and women we serve with, people who know better than anyone else what you've gone through—even talking with them isn't easy. Throw in family members who are often eager to help, but they sometimes don't realize how difficult answering even the simplest question can be.

"We're trained to lock away our emotions, to focus on the task at hand, to get the job done. Use your head and keep your heart out of it." Forrest punctured his last words with imaginary quotation marks drawn in the air. "Simple to do during the extreme moments when everything you've been taught comes as naturally as breathing, but when the job is done and things get quiet, when you're alone with your thoughts…it's a lot harder to keep your feelings under control. For some people denying any sentiment is the only way they can survive."

Annabel couldn't stop comparing Forrest's words to what Thomas had said to her as they stood in his office just a few days ago.

He'd been so adamant that there was no room in

his life for anything but his work. Somewhere along the way, he'd come to believe he couldn't have both love and his career.

In my experience, trusting in love is crazy.

Had someone taught him that? Was that why he refused to believe her when she told him how sure she was of her love for him?

"So learning to allow your feelings to be a part of your life again, that it's okay to even acknowledge the everyday emotions most people take for granted—is that what you mean?"

Forrest nodded. "I think it's a good place to start."

"So do I." For the first time in days, Annabel allowed her own emotions to flow freely, the pure joy of what she felt for Thomas to once again fill her heart.

"I'm sorry, I didn't mean to turn our talk into a personal session just for me." Forrest offered her that same slight grin as before. "See how easy it is to start jawing when this mutt of yours is around?"

"That is exactly why Smiley and I are here." Annabel reached for Forrest's hand and gave it a quick squeeze. "And I think your idea is wonderful."

"So you'll work with me on this?"

"I'd love to. We'll need to talk to people here at the hospital in order to pull it together, but I don't think that'll be a problem."

Forrest pushed himself to his feet. "You didn't let it stop you before."

"Nope." Annabel stood as well, her smile reflecting her renewed sense of confidence. Hadn't she told Thomas the first time they'd met that she could be persuasive when she wanted something? "And nothing is going to stop me this time, either."

The gravel drive crunched beneath the tires of her car as Annabel slowly pulled to a stop outside the oversize, tree-shaded building. There were only a few other vehicles in the Thunder Canyon Animal Shelter parking lot, but none that she recognized.

Was she too late?

Smiley pawed at the back of her seat when she turned off the engine. The sounds of their surroundings filtered in through the open windows.

"Yes, I know." She twisted around to look in the backseat. "You remember this place well, don't you?"

Smiley offered a low woof in response.

Removing her seat belt, Annabel got out of the car and freed Smiley, as well. She held tight to his leash as he eagerly headed for the front entrance. The office area was empty, but Annabel walked on through until they emerged back out in the bright sunshine as a familiar face met them.

"Hey there! It's good to see you two again." Betsy greeted them with a bright smile. "What brings you here this afternoon?"

"Hi, Betsy. I was hoping to find a friend of mine, but I didn't see his car out front."

"We only have one visitor here at the moment so I'm guessing that's who you're talking about. He parked around the other side in the employees' section." The woman smiled and gestured over her shoulder. "You'll find him right around the corner. Seems to be having a hard time making up his mind. Not everyone is as sure as you were that day."

Suddenly unable to speak, Annabel could only nod her thanks as she allowed Smiley to lead her to the familiar path. Rounding the corner, she stopped short at the sight in front of her.

Thomas, still dressed for work in dark slacks, a buttoned shirt now wrinkled with the sleeves folded back to his elbows, and his tie yanked halfway down his chest, sat on the grass inside a gated area, his lap overflowing with at least a dozen wiggling, happy puppies.

Three years ago, she'd come here to the Thunder Canyon Animal Shelter, drawn by a flyer advertising how a special pet could change a person's whole world. Finding Smiley within a few minutes of her arrival had been the most wonderful moment of her life…until the day the two of them walked into a certain doctor's office.

Her heart soared as she watched the ease of his smile and listened to his husky laughter as the playful pups vied for his attention. She had no idea exactly why he was here, but it was a sight she could've enjoyed for hours.

Except her pup had other ideas.

Smiley let loose with two happy yips of his own, causing Thomas and the dogs to jerk their heads their way.

"Annabel."

She offered a small wave, enchanted by the bright flush of embarrassment that crossed his features. "I'd ask if you're enjoying yourself, but that would be a silly question."

Thomas hurried to his feet, brushing at his clothes with one hand because the other cradled one petite pup in the crook of his arm. "Ah, yes. Well, you know...puppies."

"Yes, I know." She signaled for Smiley to sit. He obeyed, but that didn't stop his back end from wiggling back and forth in time with his swishing tail. "You seem to have found a new friend."

He took a few steps forward until only the wired fencing separated them, his gaze dropping for a moment to the surprisingly docile pup, whose tiny head rested contently against his chest. "I guess so."

"I didn't know you were interested in getting a dog."

His gaze returned to look at her, the icy blue coloring of his eyes reflecting a contentment she hadn't seen there before. "I guess it was a spur-of-the-moment decision."

Was that a good thing or not? Was he ready to

make more spontaneous choices in other areas of his life? And could she possibly be included in any way?

The questions filled her head, but engaging her mouth seemed impossible at the moment.

"How did you know I was here?"

Before she could answer Betsy came around the corner with a young family, complete with two boys, who seemed as excited as the puppies were to have someone new to play with.

"Hold that thought. I'd like to continue this conversation face-to-face." He waited until the shelter's director entered the gated area that allowed visitors to interact with the available pets before he slipped out and started toward her, the pup still in his arms.

To Annabel's trained eye the animal seemed to have at least some golden retriever in him, or her. She guessed the pup to be only a few months old, but the familiar coloring of its coat reminded her of Smiley when she'd first brought him home.

But it was the mixture of tenderness and purpose in Thomas's eyes that drew her gaze back to his face. Gone was the aloof detachment he'd so easily displayed in his office a few days ago.

He stopped right in front of her, leaning down to give Smiley a quick pat hello. "Hey there, Smiley." His attention returned to her. "Okay, now. How did you know where I was?"

"We were on our way to your office when we ran

into Marge at the elevator. She mentioned you'd left the shelter's website up on your computer when you left for the day." The words tumbled from her mouth, her eyes drawn to the ease with which Thomas stroked the pup's soft fur. "She, for whatever reason, thought I might like to know that."

"Of course she did."

Annabel couldn't stand it. She once again decided to jump in with both feet and trust in the love she felt in her heart and the warmth in Thomas's gaze.

"You know, I don't want to ruin a good thing. Correction, this great, amazing and wonderful thing that's happening right at this very moment, but to say I'm a bit confused is putting it mildly."

Thomas motioned toward a nearby bench. "Do you think we could sit for a moment?"

Annabel nodded, a thrill racing through her when Thomas laid his free hand at the small of her back as they made their way across the yard. Smiley sat again when she and Thomas did, his gaze moving between her, him and the pup that settled easily in Thomas's lap.

"Everything's okay, sweetie." She reassured her pet with a gentle pat, hoping the simple phrase would calm her, as well. "You can say hello."

Smiley quickly sniffed at the now-snoozing puppy then offered a low sigh before stretching out at her feet, his head resting on his paws.

"Wow, two quiet dogs. That's a bit unusual, isn't it?"

Thomas's words had Annabel returning her gaze to his. "Yes, it is, especially for a puppy. Do you have any idea what you're in for? Puppies demand a lot of time and attention. They need to be cared for, fed, bathed, trained, but most of all they need your love."

"I know all that." His smile was genuine. "I guess I've finally found the right one for me."

The whirlwind of emotions battling inside her was suddenly too much to contain. Annabel squeezed her eyes closed, but a single tear managed to escape anyway. "Thomas, you're driving me crazy here."

His touch was gentle as he cupped her jaw, his thumb brushing over her cheek to wipe the tear away. "Then the feeling is mutual. You've been nothing short of a beautiful, passionate and maddening presence in my carefully controlled world from the moment we met."

She opened her eyes. "What exactly does that mean?"

"It means my life changed in a way I never expected a few short weeks ago and as hard as I tried not to allow it to happen, you found a way past my defenses. And no matter how hard I pushed, you never gave up on me."

"I'd say that's pretty evident considering I followed you here," Annabel whispered, following her heart and all the love she carried inside for this amazing man. "I meant what I said to you three days ago. My feelings haven't changed. I love you."

This time it was Thomas who closed his eyes, his head dropping forward, pressing his forehead gently to hers. "I was so afraid I'd waited too long. That I was too late."

"Late for what?"

"To ask for another chance?" He pressed his kiss to her temple for a long moment, and then leaned back again. "Will you take a chance on me?"

Annabel's heart beat wildly in her chest. This was exactly what she wanted, what she'd hoped for when she'd decided less than a hour ago not to give up on him, but to believe in the sincerity of his words? "Thomas, you have to be sure of what you want, what you need in your life."

"I want you. I need you." He pulled her closer, his arm moving to wrap low around her waist. "I think I've known that all along. That's what was so scary, how easily you came into my life, as if you were meant to be here, with me. I love you, Annabel, and I'm going to for the rest of my life."

She laid a hand over his where it held the tiny bundle in his lap. "This...all of this is going to take a lot of hard work and commitment."

He smiled, his fingers lacing through hers. "And time, attention and love. Yeah, I got it. So, do you think you and Smiley have enough of all those things to share? For both of us? I think me and this little guy come as a package deal."

Annabel leaned forward and met Thomas's kiss while Smiley offered a resounding bark of approval. They broke apart with a shared laugh. "Two for one? How could we resist?"

* * * * *

Don't miss
REAL VINTAGE MAVERICK
by Marie Ferrarella,
the next book in the
MONTANA MAVERICKS:
BACK IN THE SADDLE *continuity.*
On sale September 2012,
wherever Harlequin books are sold.

COMING NEXT MONTH from Harlequin®
Special Edition®
AVAILABLE AUGUST 21, 2012

#2209 THE PRODIGAL COWBOY
Kathleen Eagle

Working with Ethan is more challenging than investigative reporter Bella ever dreamed. He's as irresistible as ever, and he has his own buried secrets.

#2210 REAL VINTAGE MAVERICK
Montana Mavericks: Back in the Saddle
Marie Ferrarella

A widowed rancher has given up on love—until he meets a shop owner who believes in second chances. Can she get the cowboy to see it for himself?

#2211 THE DOCTOR'S DO-OVER
Summer Sisters
Karen Templeton

As a kid, he would have done anything to make her happy, to keep her safe. As an adult, is he enough of a man to let her do the same for him?

#2212 THE COWBOY'S FAMILY PLAN
Brighton Valley Babies
Judy Duarte

A doctor and aspiring mother agrees to help a cowboy looking for a surrogate—and falls in love with him.

#2213 THE DOCTOR'S CALLING
Men of the West
Stella Bagwell

Veterinary assistant Laurel Stanton must decide if she should follow her boss and hang on to a hopeless love for him...or move on to a new life.

#2214 TEXAS WEDDING
Celebrations, Inc.
Nancy Robards Thompson

When she opens her own catering company, AJ Sherwood-Antonelli's professional dreams are finally coming true. The last thing she needs is to fall for a hunky soldier who doesn't want to stay in one place long enough put down roots....

You can find more information on upcoming Harlequin® titles, free excerpts and more at www.HarlequinInsideRomance.com.

HSECNM0812

REQUEST YOUR FREE BOOKS!

2 FREE NOVELS PLUS 2 FREE GIFTS!

⬧ Harlequin®

SPECIAL EDITION

Life, Love & Family

™ **Harlequin**®

SPECIAL EDITION

Life, Love and Family

NEW YORK TIMES BESTSELLING AUTHOR

KATHLEEN EAGLE

brings readers a story of a cowboy's return home

Ethan Wolf Track is a true cowboy—rugged,
wild and commitment-free. He's returned home to
South Dakota to rebuild his life, and he'll start by
competing in Mustang Sally's Wild Horse Training
Competition…. But TV reporter Bella Primeaux
is on the hunt for a different kind of prize,
and she'll do whatever it takes
to uncover the truth.

THE PRODIGAL COWBOY

Available September 2012 wherever books are sold!

*Enjoy an exclusive excerpt
from Harlequin® Special Edition®
THE DOCTOR'S DO-OVER by Karen Templeton*

"What I actually said was that this doesn't make sense."

She cocked her head, frowning. "This?"

His eyes once again met hers. And held on tight.

Oh. This. Got it.

Except…she didn't.

Then he reached over to palm her jaw, making her breath catch and her heart trip an instant before he kissed her. Kissed her good. And hard. But good. Oh, so good, his tongue teasing hers in a way that made everything snap into focus and melt at the same time— Then he backed away, hand still on jaw, eyes still boring into hers. Tortured, what-the-heck-am-I-doing eyes. "If things had gone like I planned, this would've been where I dropped you off, said something about, yeah, I had a nice time, too, I'll call you, and driven away with no intention whatsoever of calling you—"

"With or without the kiss?"

"That kiss? Without."

O-kaay. "Noted. Except…you wouldn't do that."

His brow knotted. "Do what?"

"Tell me you'll call if you're not gonna. Because that is not how you roll, Patrick Shaughnessy."

He let go to let his head drop back against the headrest, emitting a short, rough laugh. "You're going to be the death of me."

"Not intentionally," she said, and he laughed again. But it was such a sad laugh tears sprang to April's eyes.

"No, tonight did not go as planned," he said. "In any way, shape, form or fashion. But weirdly enough in some ways it went better." Another humorless laugh. "Or would have, if you'd been a normal woman."

"As in, whiny and pouty."

"As in, not somebody who'd still be sitting here after what happened. Who would've been out of this truck before I'd even put it in Park. But here you are..." In the dim light, she saw his eyes glisten a moment before he turned, slamming his hand against the steering wheel.

"I don't want this, April! Don't want...you inside my head, seeing how messy it is in there! Don't want..."

He stopped, breathing hard, and April could practically hear him think, *Don't want my heart broken again.*

***

Look for
THE DOCTOR'S DO-OVER
by Karen Templeton
this September 2012 from Harlequin® Special Edition®.